DRUIDS

Shelta-Thari De'Danann

LitPrime Solutions
21250 Hawthorne Blvd
Suite 500, Torrance, CA 90503
www.litprime.com
Phone: 1 (209) 788-3500

Published by LitPrime Solutions 10/07/2020

ISBN: 978-1-953397-23-2(sc)
ISBN: 978-1-953397-24-9(hc)
ISBN: 978-1-953397-25-6(e)

This book has been twenty-two years in the making and is dedicated to my beautiful little darling Ziggy, who died on Tuesday, April 4, 1995, at 6.15 p.m. She was the most wonderful little dog God ever made. I called her "my little hairy angel," and now, she truly is. She will always be in my heart and a part of my soul; I loved her so much it hurt. May God look after you and protect you, my darlin'. Your ever-loving master will forever cherish your memory.

Thanks to my lovely "little sister" Cathy in Canada, without whose friendship, encouragement, and assistance my handwritten notes (and the final chapter of this book) would never have been typed into manuscript format and sent to the publisher.

Part 1

The Coming

Chapter 1

2 October 1992

9.35 p.m.

Jesus Christ, I am sick of being a rep.

There I was, stuck in the middle of Salisbury Plain in thick, horrible fog. I'd just come from Warminster down the A36 motorway and nearly missed the turn for the A303 to Andover. I was trying to get back to the hotel my boss had booked for me. The landlady thought she was Brigitte Bardot. Maybe if it were three decades earlier and she was twenty-five years old, was a hundred pounds lighter, and didn't require peroxide to obtain that blonde hair. But never mind: it was shelter, a place to dump my stuff and lay my head down for the night.

I drove down the unfamiliar country road. There on the other side of my window, it loomed—Stonehenge. I had to pull over because visibility was dangerously low, and I was only able to see about three feet ahead of me. It was so dark, wet, and cold that I could hardly believe it. I'd spent the past eighteen hours behind the wheel, and as much as I loved to drive, I was tired, my back hurt, my hands were aching, and my eyes felt as though they were full of grit.

I had a Tab, the typical salesman's vice—well, that and booze—then went for a piss.

As I opened the car door, the cold rushed in, and I felt as though someone had just walked over my grave. For anyone else, this might have seemed weird, but being a very psychic individual myself, I didn't find it particularly unusual.

The first time I felt what I call "getting whacked" was when I was 8 years old and my nana died in my arms. Edith Anne was her name, and as her life force left her body and went on to who-knows-where, I felt a part of her come into me; all her love, affection, pain, anger, and disappointment, it all just flowed into me. As her body left this earth, her spirit filled me. That was the first time I began to understand how psychic I was. Now, more than three decades later, on my thirty-ninth birthday, after going through many transitions and getting stronger and stronger psychically, I felt as though my abilities were more of a curse than a gift.

At this point, my bladder was bursting, and the cold air only made me need to go even more. Stepping out of the car, I stood facing Stonehenge. *What a beast*, I thought, a monument to man's ingenuity, thousands of years old, towering over me like a giant.

Chapter 2

2 October 1992

10 p.m.

I walked across the grass, stopped, pulled my prick out, and let fly. The relief was tremendous. I stood there looking left and right to see if anyone was there; stupid, really, as the fog was so thick that you could hardly see in front of you, but only natural for anyone with even a hint of modesty.

The fog seemed to pulsate with an eerie glow, and Stonehenge itself seemed to disappear and reappear like something out of a *Star Trek* transporter. My piss appeared to rise like a steamy vapour and disperse into the fog, which seemed thin by comparison.

The damp and the cold gripped me with icy fingers. I shuddered, shaking off the last drops of my stream. Was it the cold, or was I getting whacked again? The sheer relief was heaven as I finished my piss and tucked my prick back in my pants. *Shit.* Why do willies always do that? No matter how much you shake them, you always get a dribble in your underpants. I stood there for a moment feeling like a fool, and as I turned to go back to the car, I got whacked hard.

I felt as though an electric pulse had been plugged into my head and switched on, rippling straight through to my toes.

I shook my head and shoulders to clear the feeling, but it felt like six tonnes of concrete weighing down on me. I quickly turned around and took stock of Stonehenge again. The glow seemed brighter as I walked towards it through the fog. Getting closer, I could see all the litter and filth around its base and, worst of all, the graffiti all over the stones. Pure sacrilege. Hippy bastards, no doubt—no respect for anything.

By this time, I was totally mesmerised by what was in front of me. I felt as though some unknown presence was lurking there, just watching and waiting. As I stood there in the dark and fog, I shuddered. *Have another Tab, Kev*, I thought.

Chapter 3

2 October 1992

10.30 p.m.

I started walking back to the road, where I could see the warning lights flashing on the car like four red-hot pokers glowing in the fog. I opened the door, sat in the driver's seat, and started up the engine. I switched the warning lights off and put the headlights and fog lights on, for all the good it did; the lights just glared back, the fog was so thick.

I pulled away slowly and crawled along at just 10 to 15 mph, which I considered a safe speed in the dense fog. I was very careful to watch for the A345 crossroads near Countess Road. *Not far now*, I thought as I carried on down the A303 to Amesbury.

I had a mini guide of Amesbury with a great little map inside, so I knew exactly where I was going. Just off the A303 was a turn-off called Stonehenge Road that took you straight into the village. Stonehenge Road bent round into Church Street, which followed straight onto the High Street to my destination, the George Hotel.

I struggled through the fog, still taking it slow, and checking my map on the passenger seat for landmarks. I saw a sign saying VESPASIAN'S CAMP, so I knew it wasn't far now. As I drove past the camp, I got whacked again. It wasn't evil, though, and I felt a warm glow as though I had seen an old friend. As I rounded the bend onto Church Street, I saw St Mary's Church looming up at me. Salisbury Street was on my left, the start of the High Street. I looked at my watch: *11.35 p.m., not bad going*, I thought. The hotel sign glowed eerily in front of me. Home at last.

I turned into the car park and put the lights on full beam to see where I was going. Not many cars. I spotted a space right next to the back door, so not as far to walk as I thought. I switched off the lights and ignition, and then breathed a sigh of relief at having got there in one piece and without an accident. I got out of the car, opened the back door, and got my books, briefcase, and rep's desk—a portable office about the size of a briefcase—off the seat. My suitcases were already at the hotel, as I had dropped them off on my way in that morning.

As I locked the door and set the car alarm, I bent down to pick up my gear, and out of the corner of my eye, I noticed a big black limousine. It was an old Rolls-Royce, complete with running boards, probably from the 1950s. It looked like a living room on wheels. *Must belong to some rich bastard*, I thought.

I turned towards the entrance to the hotel with my back to the Rolls and felt as though I was being watched. I looked back at the car, but it was so dark and foggy that I couldn't see whether anyone was there. *Bollocks*, I thought. *I'm too tired to start imagining things.*

Chapter 4

2 October 1992

11.50 p.m.

The back door of the hotel led through a hallway with a sign at the end that said RECEPTION. I walked through and approached the counter. I dropped my stuff and looked around. No one here. I could hear noises from the main bar; it sounded quite full. I pressed the buzzer and had a look around, waiting for someone to appear. The brochure said it was a sixteenth-century coaching hotel with thirty-two bedrooms, many with private facilities, TVs, and tea-making facilities, as well as public bars, hotel bars, bar snacks, and an à la carte restaurant. It was much better than most of the places I'd stayed in, but knowing my boss, I was sure mine would be the smallest, cheapest room with the bare necessities. No à la carte for me; bar snacks were all I could afford on my wage.

As I lit a cigarette, she appeared. I nearly came in my pants. She was five foot ten, slim but with a full figure, the most amazing long platinum hair right down her back, beautiful high cheekbones, a Cupid's bow mouth, and those eyes … green, oh so green, and shaped just like a cat's. She moved with absolute feline grace, her hips swaying back and forth, and her high tilted breasts, which were not too big, bounced and swayed with aquiline movement.

She stared at me standing at the reception desk, and I tingled from head to toe, icy fingers running down my back. As she came closer, all I could see were those huge green eyes with a blonde halo surrounding her face. She was a Bardot lookalike, probably what her mother had looked like thirty years ago. When I had popped in earlier that day to confirm my booking, I had met her mother. *She* had not been around, but her mother told me she'd be on the desk later.

She spoke, and I could vaguely detect that lovely Wessex dialect, but it was also very refined. "Mr D'Arcy, I presume? My name is Shelta-Thari De'Danann My mother and I own the hotel."

"My, that is some name," I said. Later, I found out exactly what her name meant, and it wasn't as exotic as it sounded. "A beautiful name for a beautiful lady," I continued.

"I've heard you Geordies [people from Newcastle-upon-Tyne] are smoothies, and it seems to be true," she replied. "Call me Shelta, for short."

"My first name is Kevin, but you can call me Kev," I replied, and she held out her long, slim hand, with perfectly manicured red nails, like talons.

As I reached for her hand, mine started to tingle, and the hairs on the back of it started to rise. When we touched, it was like static electricity; she gasped, and her large green eyes widened even further.

I stood holding her hand, and time seemed to stop. I was whacked from head to toe and felt as though some huge electrical charge was rippling through my body in a pulsating motion.

The air around her seemed to dim slightly, and I began to get what seemed like flashbacks; shapes moving around her, spectral faces moving backward and forward. There was an eerie, low chanting in the background. Her face started to change, becoming even more feline, and the first thing that came into my mind was that she looked like a snow leopard. We stood there for what seemed an eternity, but in reality, it was just a few seconds.

"Shelta-Thari," a voice boomed, and the spell was broken. I turned as if waking from a dream, and in the doorway stood a short, slim man who was muscular, wearing a perfectly tailored black tuxedo, white wing-collared shirt, and black bow tie. His jet-black hair had a blue sheen to it, and his face was so thin it looked gaunt, with a square jaw and indented cheekbones, but it was his eyes I noticed most: deep-set, black, and glaring at me with so much malevolence all he needed was a cloak. *Shit*, I thought. *Count Dracula to the rescue.*

I quickly turned back to Shelta, who was still a bit misty-eyed but seemed to have composed herself, and returned my gaze back to the man striding across the lobby toward us. His composure had completely changed. A wide grin filled his face, and his eyes, which a few seconds ago had been dark and malevolent, were now a twinkling dark purple.

"I do apologise for interrupting," the man said, "but we have a slight problem with a drunk in the bar, and I need your help, Shelta."

"Certainly," she replied. "I'll be with you in a moment, after I give Mr. D'Arcy his key."

"Good evening, Mr D'Arcy; my name is Toutaitis de la Wyle, Tony for short. I am Shelta's uncle and part owner of the hotel."

He extended his hand for me to shake, and I noticed that compared to the rest of him, his hands were almost bestial. They seemed much too large for the rest of his body, very square, very powerful, and very hairy, almost like paws.

I'd been a sales representative for years, so you get used to shaking hands; it's part of the job, but I've also done martial arts for many years, and you just sense things. I learned a trick to stop someone from crushing your hand while shaking it: set your thumb and forefinger apart in a V shape, put your hand forward palm down, and place your hand in theirs, forming a type of wedge which stops them from crushing your hand.

Tony sensed this himself but too late; I had already formed the wedge. My instincts were correct, as it was like putting my hand in a vice. As we proceeded to shake hands, his eyes twinkled like a little boy with a new toy. Our eyes locked, and he squeezed, increasing the pressure. Little did he know I had broken my hand four times before, so all the knuckles were disjointed, allowing me to bend it like putty? He smiled, and his eyes mocked me as my hand continued to fold inward. Another trick I'd learned was to let your opponent do this and absorb all his energy and strength into your own hand, then turn it back on him, a combination of your own strength and his.

I feigned pain and watched his smile spread across his ruggedly handsome features. I smiled back, and his face registered surprise. I clicked my hand back into shape, concentrated all the energy from the top of my arm, and let it flow down to my forearm. He must have felt the ripple and the roles reverse; as I did this, I kept smiling, and mute shock registered on his face. As the ripple came to my forearm, it joined with the strength I had taken from him. I then started to gently squeeze back. I call it "going down." One … the pressure started; two … harder; three, four, five, as I worked down, the pressure gradually increased. Jesus, his face was a picture. I happened to look in the mirror and saw Shelta smiling in disbelief. I reached ten and held it. Anymore, and his knuckles would have popped. His face was now set like marble, teeth clenched, and his eyes had returned to being black slits. Again, it felt like time stood still.

Fuck this for a game of soldiers, I said to myself, *it must be well after midnight now.* I'd been on the road all day. I was tired and needed to get up for an early start in the morning.

I quickly released my grip, reached for my key, and said, "Goodnight; nice to have met you, Shelta and Tony. See you in the morning." I picked up my two cases very deftly and walked towards a set of doors that said "Rooms 1 to 24." I glanced in the mirror on my way and noticed Tony staring in utter amazement, his hand slightly shaking; it might have been a trick of the light, but it looked as though his eyes now had a red tinge, and I could feel them boring into my back. I opened the door to the stairs, shuddering wearily as I made my way up each stair. Four flights later, I spotted Room 24. Bloody hell, I thought. As per usual, it was the smallest and cheapest room my boss could get, right in the attic. But when I opened the door, I got a surprise; the room was huge. It must have been thirty by twenty feet, with a huge line of windows across one wall. The curtains were closed, and I was too tired to look through them to see the view. There were two double beds, so I dumped my cases on one, undressed, and hung up my suit. I put my shirt and underwear in a bag I carried for soiled clothes, got out my toothbrush and toothpaste, and cleaned my teeth. Then I set my alarm and jumped into the bed.

I switched off the light and lit a cigarette,; I inhaled deeply and blew the smoke out in a long sigh. I thought to myself, *What a strange day. I think I'm going to have some fun here, and that Shelta.*

I visualised her naked, and my prick started to stiffen; boy, would I like to get into her knickers. I stubbed out my cigarette, lay back, and slowly drifted into oblivion.

Part 2

So It Begins

Chapter 5

3 October 1992

First day on the road. Buzzzz; the alarm went off at 7 a.m., piercing through my sleep like a knife, and I awoke with a start. "Whoa," I shouted, as I jumped up and shook my head to get rid of the cobwebs. I rubbed my eyes with my fingers, trying to clear the sleep from them. *Where am I?* I thought, noticing the unfamiliar surroundings. It began to click for me as my brain went into gear, the drowsiness now disappearing. "George Hotel, Amesbury," I said aloud. Part of the trouble with being on the road and living out of a suitcase is, you always have to keep remembering where you are.

I stretched languidly and heard all my stiffness disappear as my bones clicked back into place. Well, I say all my stiffness, but not quite; as I looked down, there was my prick standing up under the covers, like the centre pole in a circus tent. *Boy,* I thought, *that Shelta must have had some effect on me last night.* All of a sudden, in an almost dreamlike quality, I started to tingle. I detected a very sweet musky smell, almost like the scent of sex. My prick started to throb with a vengeance, and its veins swelled like mad snakes. The room started to shimmer like heat waves over a radiator, and there was a buzzing in the air. I knew what was going to happen. There was a presence near, but this early in the morning and in daylight? Strange, I thought. It was the eyes that appeared first, large and green. Shelta. Her face started to take shape in front of me. The small cute nose, then the beautiful sensuous lips, followed by that ring of gorgeous platinum curls, long and luxurious, cascading down her long slender back. Her long red nails appeared and then slowly formed into fingers and then hands, stopping at the wrist. It was like a stunning female version of the Cheshire Cat from Alice in Wonderland.

Her face was next to me, and I could smell the muskiness of her sweet minty breath. I moved back on the bed slowly, my spine coming to rest against the headboard. As I moved, I realised I had pushed back the bedclothes, and there, standing tall, proud, and throbbing like hell, was my prick. I suddenly felt her nails raking up and down my prick, very slowly and sensuously. Jesus Christ, I was having a wet dream, but I was awake.

The long slender fingers grasped my member and very slowly started to move up and down. I've heard women say that men's brains are in their trousers; well, if that's true, then I was having a haemorrhage. Her hair framed her face and shone like gossamer. As I stared at those amazing eyes, her wonderful ruby red lips smiled and then pouted. She parted her lips and then slowly ran her tongue from side to side across her top lip. Her head slowly dipped forward and then down, and as her hair cascaded down, I felt the long soft curls fall across my legs and cover them like soft wings.

Her hands stopped moving, and for a second, nothing. The old trouser snake was about to explode. *Don't stop now, for God's sake*, my brain screamed. *Oh, Jesus, what now?* I felt the tip of her tongue slowly lick my policeman's helmet, then that wonderful Cupid's bow of a mouth slowly envelope my prick, swallowing deeply. I could feel her mouth sucking as her tongue ran up the shaft, gently licking it. Then I felt her hands against my chest, pushing me back, making my back arch as her nails gently raked the flesh of my chest.

I thought I'd died and gone to heaven. This must be a dream. My mind raced.

My hands lay palm down on the bed, and my arms went rigid with the strain as she increased the pressure, pumping up and down with her head and sucking as though her life depended on it.

My groin was straining, and my balls felt like a volcano ready to erupt. Her head bobbed up and down, and her breathing was laboured. I could feel the spunk rising like an out-of-control train.

"Thar she blows," I panted.

It spurted out like a high-pressure hose; the orgasmic waves just flowed through me. *Christ, I'm going to choke her*, I thought. When the final spurt ended, she gently removed her head, looked up, and smiled, licking her lips. The spunk was still dribbling out the end of my prick, and then she dipped her head again, grabbed hold of my prick with her left hand, and licked it off like a lollipop. When she had licked it dry, she raised her head, gently touched my face with her right hand, smiled, and pouted me a kiss. She winked her eye and then disappeared. Bloody hell. I've heard of the phantom wanker, but this took the biscuit. I stood up on shaking legs. My mind was racing with the Bryan Adams song, "I Think I've Died and Gone to Heaven."

I went into the bathroom and had a shower. Afterwards, I looked at my reflection in the mirror as I applied the shaving foam. *Not a bad face*, I thought. Square, black moustache with slight grey streaks that matched my short hair (which was slightly thinning on top), thin lips (hence, the moustache), medium-sized nose, and deep set brown eyes which changed colour according to my mood: normally brown, slightly greenish brown when I'm happy and black when I'm annoyed. I've been told I have a hypnotising stare.

After showering, I laid out my underwear, socks, shirt, tie, suit, and shoes. I put on my underwear and socks, then dabbed my face with Joop aftershave. God, it's lush; what an amazing smell, and the girlies love it. I sprayed some deodorant under my arms and then on my feet, adding a small amount down the John Thomas area. As I put my shirt on, I studied my torso. Not bad for nearly forty, I thought, considering all the dodgy food I eat and the fact that I'm just sitting and driving round all day. I'm nearly six feet tall and thirteen stone (which is considered healthy for my height). I have a slight paunch, but don't we all? I always wear double-breasted suits, since they hide my slight beer belly. I'm fortunate because I always appear to have a bit of a tan; it gives me a slightly foreign look, so I can get away with wearing any colour.

One of my sisters had nicknamed me Burt, as in Burt Reynolds, because she said I looked like him. She also said I had very broad forearms, not quite Popeye but firm and hard; probably has a lot to do with all the driving and steering the car. I do have quite powerful hands, fairly small for a man but square and stubby, and I always keep them clean and well manicured. People in the advertising game always look at hands; they seem to denote people's character. Not only that, but the ladies like a man to look good and smell nice; they hate dirty hands and fingernails.

I put some clear gel on my hands and rubbed it in, let it dry for a couple of minutes, then brushed it back to help hide the thinning area. I'm no Rab C. Nesbitt, because it's only at the back, but it gives me a fuller look. The grey bits at the side gleam, and it gives me a more distinguished, elegant appearance. The brand-new Ben Sherman shirt next; they're lovely shirts, thick white cotton with a button-down collar; my red silk patterned tie went on after that. Then I sprayed some deodorant on my shirt and in the armpits of my jacket, just to keep it smelling fresh. I put on my black suit with a thin red pinstripe, double-breasted, with six pleats in the trousers and turn-ups next, followed by my black slip-on brogues. They cost me eighty pounds but were worth every penny; they fit like a dream; I've always liked comfortable shoes while I'm driving. My monogrammed silver Cross pen gets placed in my inside jacket pocket, and the red silk patterned hanky matching my tie gets tucked into the outside pocket. Next, the gold and diamond Sekonda watch that looks a bit like a Rolex, simple and elegant but nothing too flashy; ensemble complete. I make a quick check in the mirror for any unsavoury fluff or marks; nope.

Boy, you look the business, I thought.

Seven Bellies (that is my boss, Jim Rowan) says it's all about first impressions in our game; the client weighs you up in the first thirty seconds, so look good, but not flashy like a car salesman.

I pick up my key, briefcase, and rep's desk, making sure everything's turned off as I headed towards to the door. Whoops; the curtains were still closed. Might as well have a look at the view, I thought.

When I opened the curtains and looked out, I was amazed. We must have been over a hundred feet high, and the view was spectacular. To my left was Amesbury Park, and to the right of that was the abbey, a Gothic monstrosity. In the distance was Stonehenge Road winding to the north-west, and a little farther away, you could see Stonehenge, tall and proud, in all her mystical glory. It gleamed in the sunlight like a mirage from the past and looked so calm and serene, compared to the night before in the thick fog and darkness. *When I get back tonight,* I thought, *I'll go back and have a look at it in the moonlight; it must be something to see.*

I don't eat breakfast; somehow it doesn't agree with me, so time for my coffee injection. I pick up my cases, shut and lock the door, and then make my way down to reception. Bottom of the stairs, turn left, here we are. As I approach the desk, Shelta appears, as if by magic.

"'Morning, Mr. D'Arcy. Did you enjoy your sleep?" she enquires, and then smiles and licks her lips, just like the apparition did about an hour ago.

Whoa, here we go again with the tingles. She'd noticed my obvious discomfort and I could feel myself blushing. She seemed to look at me knowingly and smiled again mischievously. "Morning, Shelta," I said, "and please call me Kev. Mr D'Arcy seems so formal, and since we know each other intimately now, I don't think we should have another cock-up." *Stick that up your tattie*, I thought. She smiled again, that cheeky glint in her eye. "You never know how many rises I'll get today, do you?" I continued.

"Well, aren't we in a good mood this morning, Kev?" she asked in her low husky voice, which just oozed sensuality.

"Well, yesterday was my birthday, and I missed out on celebrating it, driving down here and finding my way round. I'm finished early today, so later this afternoon, I'm going to celebrate. If you fancy joining me, I'd be most grateful. I hate drinking alone."

"I finish at five and can meet you in the cocktail lounge," she replied, with no hesitation at all.

I walked out the door and into the car park, and there she was: the Big White Super Bitch. No, not a monster; it's the nickname I gave my car, a diamond white Sierra Sapphire two-litre LXI. She's a German import with a full Cosworth body kit, comprised of a font spoiler with lights on, back spoiler on the boot, and full side skirts. The tinted windows set all of this off and made it look like a right beast. I practically live in my car, and being self-employed, I do own it, so it's like a mobile office on wheels. The interior is black leather, which sets if off nicely, and it has electronic everything: windows, sunroof, quad stereo, on-board computer, the lot. It's more like a living room on wheels.

Being a bit of a poser anyway, I'd added a few extras: hands-free car phone, laptop computer, and a portable fax machine, all linked up to my rep's desk. A little invention of my own stored all my paper files and acted as a desk next to me on the passenger seat. All in all, she was a hell of an impressive machine, and when you pull up outside a client's office you get noticed, which is exactly what you want, because you look all business. You're there to do business. Again, it's all about impressions in this game.

I opened the passenger door, placed my rep's desk in the well near the passenger seat, and fixed the straps to stop it sliding around. I set my briefcase on the back seat. The central locking clicked as I opened the driver's door, disconnecting one of three alarms I have in the car. I sat down in the Reccaro driver's seat that caresses you like your mother's arms. I've got to be comfortable since I drive a thousand miles a week, on average. The centre console and armrest in between the seats allowed me to store tapes, money, and all sorts. A small computer keypad built into the dash is where I enter the code to disconnect the second alarm. Last, but not least, I place the key in the immobiliser, disconnecting the third and final alarm.

Now, you might think this all a bit over the top, but scum nowadays will nick anything, and the Big White Super Bitch is a prime target, so anything to stop the bits of shit (as I call them) will do. If I had my way, I'd wire it up to electrocute them if they tried to nick it, the bastards; let 'em fry.

I placed the ignition key in the slot and turned it. Straight away, the double-overhead-cam, fuel-injected engine kicked into life.

The rev counter climbed as I gently touched the throttle, and it growled and purred like a caged lioness. The sports exhaust gives the engine a deep, throaty rumble, like a North American muscle car. As the electronics lit up and switched on, all you could hear was bleep, bleep, bleep as they reset themselves; it looked more like the flight deck of an airplane than the dashboard of a car. After the engine warmed up, the revs dropped, and it began to purr like a Rolls-Royce.

God, I love this car so much; if it had hair 'round the exhaust pipe, I'd shag it.

I slipped it into first gear, and she gently eased away, then into second, and indicated left; nothing was coming, so I carried on down the High Street onto Church Street, shifted into third, and followed the road round to the right, merging onto Stonehenge Road. The road was clear, so I eased up into fourth, and the engine growled again; it loves to motor. As I approached 70 mph, I slipped it into fifth, and a David Bowie lyric came to mind: "Ground control to Major Tom …" The Big White Super Bitch or, TWSB for short, glided along effortlessly; she loved power, and you could hear her purring with delight. I know it sounds silly, but spending so much time in a car, you grow attuned to it. You form a connection with it, knowing what it can and cannot do, all of its little foibles. I believe everything has a Manitou, a soul or spirit of good or evil, in it, and your chemistry, like lovers, can match. The TBWSB and I had this chemistry.

The only thing you have to watch is your speed, as it is so quiet when motoring, you can be doing over 100 mph before you know it. Once night, I was coming back from Dover, on my way to Carlisle in Cumbria (that's where the company is based). I had been stuck in nearly every traffic jam in Great Britain on the way back. I was on the M6 going north; nothing was on the road as I came past Blackpool, so I put my foot down on the accelerator.

Tubular Bells 2, one of my favourite driving CDs, was blasting out of the four speakers. The dashboard was lit up like the flight deck of a Concorde, giving the car a warm glow. Outside was pitch-black as I was coming into the Lakes, so it gave a false optical illusion of what was going on outside. I was singing to myself, as you do, and glanced down at the speedo. Well, fuck me sideways: I was doing 137 mph, and my foot still wasn't flat down on the pedal. I nearly shit myself. As I throttled down, it gave me the impression of a plane flying through the night and coming in to land. What surprised me the most was, TBWSB loved it, like a gigantic jaguar let loose. That night, I learned to never underestimate her power. I know I've rambled on for a bit about TBWSB, more than I should. I'm not showing off; as you will read later on, all this wonderful harnessed power and her Manitou really kicks in with a vengeance. And without going into graphic detail about her, you'd never understand. But I bet many readers will understand the rapport you get with your car. She was cruising at 70 mph (the legal limit, which I always try to stick to) when Chris Rea's "Road to Hell" started blasting out the radio. As I headed towards Wyle on the A303, I thought, *God, I hope this is not an omen*. Boy was I right.

I glanced down at the fax machine, which was printing out my first appointment for nine o'clock. I had calculated it was about thirteen miles from Amesbury, and I usually timed it at a mile a minute, driving at 60 mph. I arrived at 8.40. Mr John Tobias, The Willows, Wyle was the address I was looking for: bloody typical of my boss, Jim Rowan (we call him Seven Bellies because he is a five-foot, six-inch cuboid; his bellies hang over his trousers, as he is nearly sixteen stone). Seven Bellies hadn't put a street name or directions, but thankfully, there was a telephone number.

Let me explain how the system works. Many salesmen will sympathise with what I'm about to tell you, as it is every rep's nightmare. Our company sells advertising space all over Great Britain for a trade magazine called *Workforce*. This publication is a way of getting tradesmen, builders, plumbers, joiners, and so on to advertise with our company, for a fee, of course. Once they sign up, we advertise their business in *Workforce*, which is sent round to all the private housing within a fifteen-mile radius. Residents then use this like a reference book to find trades people who have been screened and vetted by us to show they are honest and reliable. Hopefully, they will then use them instead of getting a cowboy to do a job and having no recourse, if anything goes wrong. It is fairly successful nationwide, and we can quote other areas where we've done this. The problem is the bullshit you get from the telesales staff. They arrange the appointments and pick the designated area, in this case Salisbury, and start ringing builders, working from A downwards, to arrange appointments, any day from Monday to Friday, 9 a.m. to 7.30 p.m. There's a ninety-minute gap between each appointment. They then give the prospective client the spiel and patter on how good

Workforce is, all the features and benefits of how it will enhance their trade, but they rarely mention prices (that is up to me to confirm how big or small they want their advertisement and price it accordingly). The telesales are then supposed to get a time and day that suits the client for me to see them and confirm the address and telephone number and get any other information (e.g., up above a shop, next to a church or pub), as it makes it easier for the rep to find them. The reason being we are strangers in the area and driving round at night and looking for addresses in the dark is a nightmare.

Sounds easy, doesn't it? Well, let me tell you what normally happens. The telesales, in my case Les Kent, Wurzel for short (I give nicknames to everyone who bugs me; it helps eliminate the pressure), rings them and gives them the bare, bare information. "Oh, it's okay, sir. Mr D'Arcy will explain in graphic detail when he comes to see you" is his usual patter. This is because he's a lazy bastard, and I end up doing all the work. He then repeats the address and telephone number and asks if it's correct. Screw any directions to find the place. "Mr D'Arcy will find it, no problem whatsoever. He's a very experienced salesman" is his way of getting out quick before the client can ask any more questions, so he can get on to the next punter, as he is paid for getting appointments. This is what we call in the trade "blagging them in."

So the poor rep is left to struggle round, trying to find a place, and when you get there eventually (thank God for mobile phones, as telesales were supposed to get in the first place), you spend nearly half your time (there is ninety minutes between each appointment, e.g., 9 to 10.30 a.m.) explaining who you are, what you are, and why you are here. Ring any bells, girls and boys? Well, I am sure it does.

But Wurzel's favourite trick is blagging them in when the client isn't interested. "Oh, it's okay, Mr Whatever, Mr D'Arcy is always in the area, so it is no problem for him to pop in and see you, as he is passing anyway" is his fave routine. I struggle like hell racing against the clock and struggle to find the place, and then we get blown away, which means "I told your Mr Kent that I wasn't interested, but he said you would be passing anyway and then put the phone down. So I'll tell you to your face: I don't want any," and that is that.

Well, girls and boys, I bet that one hits home also. That's Les for you, but to conjure up even more pictures, as these are all key characters, let me describe the Supreme Being. Yes, like it or not, that is how he describes himself. He is tall, slim, and very wiry, and he has a full head of straw-coloured hair; this is very apt for Wurzel. The only trouble is, he looks as though he stuck his finger in an electric socket, as it goes haywire. As for dress sense, he makes Wurzel Gummidge look like Pierre Cardin. He has charge accounts in every charity shop in Cumbria. Features, well, if I say he has a face like a burglar's dog chewing a wasp, how is that for a picture in your mind?

But the one thing about Les Kent, Supreme Being, is the smell. To give you a simile (get the plastic bags ready), he smells like a septic abscessed pile cooking in a microwave on full power. Now if that is a Supreme Being, I'm pleased that I am just a simple man. To any ladies reading the book, I apologise, but you now understand part of who and what I am working with.

As the Chris Rea song finishes, I see a sign up ahead saying "Wyle." First thing I look out for is another person to talk to and ask for directions to the Willows. Not a soul in sight. Look for a post office is my next usual course. As I drive slowly round, I see they are all beautiful cottages, very olde world. A little piece of heaven, as it looks like time has stood still for a couple of hundred years.

All of a sudden, I see a squat female figure coming out of a cottage; her back is to me, and she's pulling an old-fashioned buggy-type pram. I indicate to pull over to the left and start to slow down; pressing the button for the electric window on the passenger side (the windows are deeply tinted, so you cannot see in). I drew up next to her and stop.

“Excuse me,” I say in my best posh Geordie voice.

She stops and turns to the right to face me. Her hair was shortish, thick and dark brown, just hanging over her face, so it was slightly obscured as she turned and looked me in the eye. Considering what had happened earlier on that morning, I still had a picture of Shelta’s face in my mind, but nothing on earth could have prepared me for the face I was looking at now. In my game, you are ready for anything. It’s like being an actor on the stage. This came out of one of West Craven’s nightmares. She was female by gender only; this was Quasimodo reincarnated as a woman. This was no accident victim; this was like genetic engineering had gone through a nuclear holocaust.

The first thing I thought of was, she looks like Charles Laughton in *The Hunchback of Notre Dame* in drag. My face never flinched or registered surprise, and I did my best Burt Reynolds lookalike smile and said, “Excuse me, love [Geordies always say “love” or “pet,” but I thought “pet” was a bit cruel], but I’m looking for Mr Tobias at the Willows.

“That’ll be right,” she responded. “I’m Mrs Tobias, and this is the Willows.”

The voice that answered me had no right to be in that body. Again, it had that lovely Wessex lilt to it, but it sounded so young and melodic. It was in sharp contrast to what stood before me.

“Good morning, Mrs Tobias; my name is Kevin D’Arcy from *Workforce.* I have a nine o’clock appointment with your husband, and I believe he is expecting me.”

“Know nothing about it; don’t tell me and young John a thing,” she replied, and as if by some mystical command, when his name was mentioned, young John cried. She bent down and picked the baby up from the buggy, which I noticed, was an old-fashioned design but looked as though it was newly made. Shocked and stunned again, to quote Billy Connolly, this baby was amazing.

"Sorry," said Mrs Tobias, "but he is only one and teething."

I have a niece, Gemma; she is one (but more about her later), and obviously a little girl was nothing in comparison to what she held in her arms. He looked at least two and a half years old; with a thick mop of blond hair and the most piercing blue eyes I've ever seen. Young John stopped crying as soon as he was picked up; he turned and stared straight at me. *Fuck me*, I said to myself, and I must have visibly shuddered, as I got whacked yet again. These weren't the eyes of a one-year-old. These eyes were wise eyes, wise beyond their years; it made him look like a sixty-year-old dwarf.

Regaining my composure I asked, "Is it okay to park here and go and give your husband a knock?"

"Course you can; go round the side and he'll be in the workshop in the back. Nice car; looks like something from out of space. Don't see many like that round here."

She looked at all the gadgets as the fax had started printing out again, and the mobile phone was ringing. I didn't answer the phone, as it would only be Seven Bellies, harassing me to death. Anyway, the answering service would take a message.

She put the baby back and started to walk away. "Thanks very much, Mrs Tobias," I shouted through the window. "Have a nice day,"

"That'll be right," she said. "My name is Dorcas. We'll meet again, Kev."

She disappeared up the road as I gathered my props, as I call them. I thought, *What a nice lady, and isn't God unkind to deform this person so badly but give her such a beautiful voice.*

Voice, my mind screamed. *Voice, talk, hold on a fucking minute; she called me Kev.* I said Kevin D'Arcy. No, no, you mad Geordie bastard; it's only a coincidence. Little did I know that it wasn't?

I picked up my briefcase and locked the doors; I only used the one alarm on the central locking when I was parked outside a client's; either way, if the alarm went off, the whole of Wessex would hear the sirens going and see the lights going, hear an activated tape saying, "Stop. I am being stolen; call the police." and the number plates dropping down and lighting up with the words "I have been stolen." All in all, enough to deter any piece of scum from touching TBWSB. She didn't like being molested by anyone; just like any lady, she only liked her partner, which was me.

The cottage was gorgeous, all wood and thatched. Vines were all over it and those beautiful leaded Tudor-type windows. I made my way round the side of the cottage and down the path to the back garden and workshop.

The workshop looked like a small barn, with double doors in the front. There were piles of timber all over: all shapes, sizes, and colours. The man was a carpenter and master joiner, so it was only to be expected. The back garden looked dark in comparison to the front garden, and as I looked up, I saw the reason why. Towering nearly eighty feet high, overshadowing the workshop, was a huge oak tree, blotting out nearly everything from the mid-morning sun. I am no expert, but I imagine it must have been a few centuries old.

As I approached the workshop doors, they opened. You older people might remember a song about a mining disaster. It was called "Big John," and the chorus went, "His name is John, Big John, Big Bad John." Well, this song could have been written for him.

The song said he was a giant of a man. Well, so was this John. He stood six foot, eight, if he was an inch. Everything was in proportion:

huge blond shaggy head, with the piercing blue eyes, arms like my legs, a huge barrel chest, and legs like tree trunks; young John was a clone of his father. His body was slightly tanned, obviously fading as winter approached, and he was very muscular. You could see every contour and every line, his body honed to perfection. His eyes glared at me (but not like young John's) as they adjusted to the different light variations from the workshop into the semi-daylight.

Lights, stage, action, my best Burt Reynolds smile: "Good morning, Mr Tobias. Kevin D'Arcy from *Workforce*. I believe we have a nine o'clock appointment." I always say that because I have been to see so many people, and they say, "No, we haven't," or "It isn't today but tomorrow," or something else like that. That is how much faith I have in Wurzel.

"That'll be right, Mr D'Arcy, is it?" he replied in a deep baritone voice. He had obviously forgot that I just introduced myself as Kevin D'Arcy; never mind. "Just brewed a pot of tea; would you like a cup?" he asked.

Great, a good start, remembered my name, sort of, and offered me a drink, so it's a foot in the door, as we salesmen say. Still smiling, I offered my hand to shake his. He offered his, another good sign. I was amazed; his hands were quite small compared to the rest of him, but he had long slim fingers, just like a piano player. I had expected it to be hard and calloused, but it was surprisingly soft. If you had reversed hands with him and Tony de la Wyle, then it would have been a perfect match. Tony, slim and elegant with hands like paws, and this giant of a tradesman with hands like a piano player; curiouser and curiouser.

As he put his hand in mine, he said, "No funny tricks now."

Don't panic, Kev, I told myself. This was getting weird. I know what village grapevines are like. I come from the north-east, a lovely little town called Whitley Bay. I live in West Monkseaton, which is like a suburban village; everyone in the local pub, the Hunting Lodge, knows the far end of a fart and which way it blows. But for news to travel this fast, especially since the episode with Tony only happened at midnight last night, dah dah dah dah, "The Twilight Zone" sprung to mind.

"How do you take it?" John asked.

"Milk and two sugars, please," I replied.

As I watched him make the brew, I looked around the workshop. This man was an artist, a Michelangelo; the things I saw were works of art. Sculptures of animals, birds, and people were almost lifelike. There were Gothic-type carvings all around for churches or mansions or the like. Three statues like his wife's stood there. One just a basic carcass, another one almost complete, and the last one finished, just waiting to be varnished. He handed me my mug of tea.

"Thanks, Mr Tobias," I said.

"Call me John, Kev," and smiled as he said it. Dah dah dah dah, dah dah dah, the tune to "The Twilight Zone," plays in my head again.

"Okay, John; that's very kind of you."

"We are all very kind round here, if treated right."

Am I getting paranoid, or were there subtle overtones there? I smiled at him and in my mind said *Fuck you, you sheep-shagging interbred bastard.* They can't do you for your thoughts. His eyes flinched. *Shit, or can they?* Came my own reply.

Always flatter the client, says Seven Bellies. Praise his house, work, or office, or whatever the punters revel in.

"You have some superb articles, John; truly remarkable. You must have a God-given talent.

He smiled and replied, "Depends which God."

Is this some kind of fucking test? His eyes twinkled as if he had read my mind again. Keep calm Kev I said. "How's business then, John?" I asked, starting my spiel.

"Been alright for the last three hundred years," Came the reply. Another Wurzel blowout, a mushroom cloud from an atomic bomb smoke appeared in my head.

"I take it Mr Kent told you all about *Workforce* on the phone and how it can benefit your business?" I continued, pushing my patter.

"Told me very little; rambled on that you'd be in the area and would explain it all to me when you came. Told him I wasn't interested, but he wouldn't take no for an answer. So I thought if you are already here anyway, you might like a cup of tea for your trouble and then be on your way."

My mind started reeling; you stupid fuck, pig human bastard, Kent. Fucked it up again; blagged it in to look good to Seven Bellies, then I get the blame for not getting the sale. No point in prolonging the agony; if he had been here for three hundred years, he'd have this place sewn up tighter than a nun's knickers, so get out gracefully.

"Well, obviously, there is no point in going any further, John; thank you for the tea, and good luck."

"Don't need good luck. It is all mapped out; always has been, always will be. See you soon, Kev."

John stood up and towered over me, even after I got out of my chair. I extended my hand, and as I went to shake his, he pulled sharply back.

"No tricks now," he said, laughing out loud in a deep baritone guffaw.

I walked back up the path towards the front of the house. "Shit, fuck, and cacky [more shit in Geordie]," I muttered under my breath.

I turned and glanced in the front window; it looked like a front living room, and there on the inside window sill was a family photograph. Big John, young John in the arms of a very small pretty woman. I stared, mesmerised. Can this be Dorcas, Mrs Tobias? If so, something had gone wrong. Young John looked about six months old, so what the hell had happened in six short months?

I'm supposed to ring into the office after every sale to let them know whether I got the business or not. If I did get the sale, Seven Bellies would whoop up and down with glee. If the reverse happened, no excuses because Wurzel fucked up with all his bullshit; it was my fault. I was useless; "Call yourself a salesman?" is what you got. And I really wasn't in the mood.

I opened the car door, put my briefcase on the seat, slid into the driver's seat, and shut the door. I switched on the ignition, and the radio came on; all the lights flashed as the machines reset themselves.

I looked at the fax; my next appointment was at noon in Larkhill, which was right next to Stonehenge. I turned the key in the ignition, and TBWSB jumped into life, I let her idle for a few seconds so she could warm up.

Bugger the radio, I thought and put *God's Great Banana Skin* in the CD player. I selected track 3, which is the title track. If you haven't heard it, it's the business (that means good in Geordie). The words are superb, and the music itself always cheers me up and makes me smile. As I headed up the A303 towards the A360 to Larkhill, Chris Rea's deep bass voice was singing, "When that man in the sky points his finger at you, don't you ever think no one's better than you. God's Great Banana Skin, gonna get you."

Very prolific, I thought. Just before the turn-off for Larkhill, Stonehenge appeared on the left, in all her majesty. Being mid-winter, the tourist trade was at low ebb, but there were three or four vehicles parked up. I saw a caterer's van by the side of the car park; you know, the sort Greasy Joe's, tea, coffee, burgers, and so on. Time for another coffee injection, my body said. TBWSB cruised into the car park, probably looking like something out of *Close Encounters of the Third Kind.* The diamond white of her paintwork gleamed, as I always kept her washed and polished. The dark tinted windows made a strange contrast, as you couldn't see inside the car; it looked like there was no driver. I saw tourists turn and look. Nearly everywhere I went, people did look at TBWSB. She was what car magazines call a real head-turner. I stopped next to the burger van and got out. Now if I do say so myself, I cut quite a dash in my working clothes; people seem to think I'm well off. Not true; "the best-dressed pauper in Whitley Bay" is what I say to my friends, but the effect of being well off is what I want to create.

"Morning," I said to the pretty, petite, dark-haired girl behind the counter. "Coffee, white with two sugars, please."

After she prepared the coffee, she said, "That'll be 65p, please."

I gave her a pound coin, and she handed me the change.

"Thanks," I said as I picked up my change. As I started to walk back to the car, a voice said, "You'll be Kev then," and I turned and realised it was the burger girl talking to me. Marvin Gaye's "Heard It through the Grapevine" started playing in my head.

"That'll be right," I mimicked, as I'm quite a good impressionist. "News travels fast round here."

"Well, there aren't any cars like yours floating round the Salisbury area, so it had to be you." She giggled like a little girl. She reminded me of a cheeky little elfin.

I was just about to give her some of my famous Geordie patter when I heard the fax machine start again. I opened the passenger door and sat on the seat, click click. "KEVIN!" started to appear on the sheet. Oh fuck, Seven Bellies is in a bad mood. I knew this as he always called me Kev, and I could hear his smarmy Cumbrian voice drawling out "Kevin."

The fax continued, "It is now 10.15 a.m., and you haven't answered your phone." Then in big bold letters (like he was shouting), "FUCKING RING ME NOW." I could see his fat bulbous, nearly bald, toothless head, grimacing as it normally did. Now as you all know, mobile phones are notorious for signal variations; you can watch the signal strengths go up and down all the time, and sometimes, they just cut out altogether. Being a Geordie, I play on this just to annoy Seven Bellies.

"What? Sorry, Jim; I can't hear you. It's is a bad reception."

I have said that many times as the line crackles away. When the signal meter goes to 1, switch off, disconnect, and there is nothing he can do about it. It is my way of annoying him and not talking to him.

A spare piece of A5 paper was lying in my briefcase, so I picked it up and wrote, "Very bad reception down here, Jim; will try to ring after 12 o'clock appointment; it just depends what the signal is like further up the road. Regards, Kev."

I placed the paper in the fax machine and pressed the autodial number. The sheet slowly disappeared into the machine, the message winging its way to Carlisle. It should keep him appeased for a while. I slowly sipped my coffee; it tasted like nectar. I put my coffee down on the desk, got up, and shut the passenger door. I walked round to the driver's side, opened the door, and sat down behind the steering wheel. "Back in the cockpit" was my expression.

My diary sat there, and I picked it up: "12 noon, Mr Graham Hood, 16A High Street, Larkhill, TV and Video Engineer," followed by the phone number. That's more like it; a guy I could talk to, as by now you've worked out that I love my music and gadgets, so we should have a lot in common.

TBWSB roared into life as I switched her on. Engine growling (as I deliberately throttled it a bit more than usual), and the sports exhaust made it sound like a souped-up racing car. What a show-off. Well, if you got it, flaunt it, is my motto. I spun TBWSB round and turned towards the burger van; I pulled up beside it and pressed the button for the driver's electric window. It whirred down, letting the light into the car; the entire interior lit up, showing all the gadgets on display. As I handed the burger girl back the coffee cup, I could see she was impressed, as her dark elfin eyes opened wide.

"Thank you, that was lovely," I said. "See you again sometime."

"That'll be right," she replied.

Cruising along the A360 to Larkhill, I noticed on my map there was a symbol for an information centre; that had to be the High Street, and Mr Hood's should be somewhere near. Larkhill, the sign said, and underneath was a sign with an "i," denoting information, pointing right. Magic, nice and easy to find. This is better, I thought, as I saw people of all shapes, sizes, and colours milling round the High Street. A neon blue sign stood out above a shop on the right: "G. Hood, TV and Video Engineer" shone brightly. Mr Hood's van stood outside in a lay-by, and there was a space right next to him, where I parked. TBWSB is nearly eleven feet long, but with the power steering, it is easy to park. "Pay and Display," it said on a sign. I got out of the car, and the pay machine was next to Mr Hood's van. Fifty pence for one hour, it said, so I put 50p in, got the ticket, went back to the car, and stuck it on the windscreen. I picked up my briefcase and clicked a switch on the dashboard. As I turned the key in the central locking, the alarm set, and a female voice said, "Please do not touch this car; I am fully alarmed." Yes, another gadget; flash, aren't I? People stopped and stared at the car and then me. I smiled and walked into the shop.

A man was standing there, laughing his head off at the scene outside the shop. In a lovely Welsh accent, he said, "Well, that is some show; if you want to get noticed round here, you have certainly done that. It'll be all over the area like wildfire.

"Mr Hood, I presume? Kevin D'Arcy from *Workforce*. I believe we have a twelve o'clock appointment."

"Pleased to meet you," Mr Hood said. "That's the best laughter I have had in a long time." He vigorously pumped my hand as he shook it. "And please, call me Graham."

"Nice to meet you, Graham; please call me Kev."

"Coffee or tea?" Graham asked.

"Not for me, thanks, I just had one, but I would like to use your loo, if I may," I asked politely.

"First door on your right, just follow your nose."

A sense of humour, I thought to myself, laughing. *I think I am going to enjoy this.*

As I walked back in to the shop, Graham was lighting up a cigarette, another social leper, thank God for that. You'd be surprised how many clients won't let you smoke, and as all us smokers know, it eases the tension.

"Do you mind if I join you?" I asked.

"Here, have one of these," Graham said, offering me his pack.

"Cheers," I said.

As I lit up, Graham was switching off his soldering iron. *Good*, I thought, *that means he wants to talk*. You notice all these things when you are in sales. You read body language and get the vibes, good or bad; all these signs were good. Graham was about my height, slim but with a slight paunch, a bit of middle-age spread, as he was about fiftyish. He was bald on top, but like most of us who lose our hair, it was cut short at the back and sides so it didn't look like Max Wall when you try to grow it longer. He had smiling brown eyes and was very congenial, like most Welshmen, a kindred spirit to Geordies who are very similar in background. Yet I sensed an air of authority and agility. Putting two and two together, the muscular frame, the authoritative, air and the electronics, I guessed ex-forces.

"Staying local?" Graham asked.

"George Hotel, Amesbury," I answered.

"Nice there, been in for a couple of drinks, but being an outsider, they keep themselves to themselves."

Outsider; typical country yokels, I thought.

"I take it Mr Kent told you all about *Workforce* then?" I asked, launching into my spiel.

"Don't bother Kev," answered Graham. *Shit*, I thought, *another blowout*, but then Graham continued, "It sounds great. The local papers round here are crap, and they charge a fortune; they have the monopoly, so *Workforce* is exactly what I've been looking for. Mr Kent didn't give me any idea of prices, but I like the concept."

Oh, joy and happiness, a man with sense and hardly any selling to do. Presenter open, I showed Graham all the artwork layouts and explained the prices of the ads according to size and frequency. He showed me his company logo and an advert he usually ran in the *Amesbury Gazette.* I did some rough designs, as I'm a designer as well, and Graham loved it, as I put in some new advertising gimmicks as well. He took a half-page spread, which cost six hundred pounds (this counted as two sales, as a quarter-page was one). I was happy, as this made up for the one I had lost with John Tobias. I hoped this would keep Seven Bellies happy. I decided since he was such a nice guy, and he paid cash (Seven Bellies would come in his pants with joy; he hated payment by cheque, as clients could change their mind after you leave and cancel the cheque), that I would put him on the inside front page so he'd be one of the first ads you saw. That was good for business, and I also gave him a free entry into the emergency numbers section, usually used for twenty-four-hour plumbers, glaziers, and so on. I decided I liked this man, and he seemed lonely. Outsider came to mind again.

As I shook his hand and thanked him, I said, "I've got an early finish today, as it was my birthday yesterday. I noticed in your ad that you finish at 5.30, and since I'm an outsider too, I was wondering if you'd like to come to the George and have a drink with me tonight and help me celebrate. I can put most of the drinks on expenses, tax deductible, as you know."

His face lit up with a cheeky boyish grin, and he looked ten years younger. "Does 7.30 p.m. suit you?" he asked.

"Fine, I'll meet you in the cocktail bar then." I shook his hand again and walked to the car.

My watch said 12:59 and 30 seconds as I put the key in the door of TBWSB, just as a male traffic warden came walking towards me, book in hand. He looked like a hobbit out of Tolkien's *Lord of the Rings*.

"Bloody hell, he is keen," I said, as I stepped into the car. I sat down, flicked the switch on the talking alarm, and put the key in the ignition, switching it on. TBWSB's voice, as I called it, boomed out, "This car is now disarmed; move back, please, as we are ready to move."

The hobbit's jaw dropped in sheer amazement, and TBWSB's engine gave a guttural, groaning throb, as if she sensed danger. I got whacked again. The hobbit's piggy slit eyes narrowed as though he was approaching some wild beast; little did the little shite know, and just for spite, as I put her in reverse for a quick getaway (12:59 and 58 seconds). I revved hard, for one little second. TBWSB sounded like some prehistoric dinosaur in a temper. The hobbit physically jumped back. I reversed and pulled back, indicated left, and started to pull away. Past one o'clock, as I put her in first gear and started to pull away. I pressed the button for the driver's window, and it eased down.

Pulling away, I smiled at the hobbit and said, "Have a nice day, and by the way, I hope you eventually find your Mam and Dad" (that is a posh Geordie way of calling you a bastard).

A quizzical look came over the hobbit's face as his one brain cell kicked into gear, and then the look of surprise as that individual gave him the answer to my sarcastic remark. All I could see in my mirror as I pulled away was the hobbit glaring at me with venom, and him standing there, shaking with sheer rage. Methinks I've made an enemy; I had better watch myself. Mystic Meg couldn't have made a better prophecy.

Suddenly, 01461332538 came up on the screen of the mobile phone as I pressed memory 1, Workforce, on the dialling pad.

"Hello, *Workforce,* Supreme Being here, Came the dulcet tones of Wurzel through the phone speaker".

Now I didn't tell you before, but Wurzel talked quite posh, so you'd have no idea listening to him that he was a walking, stinking, dung heap.

"Cut the shit, Les," I said into the hands-free microphone (God I love this car).

"Well, what happened to your nine o'clock?" Wurzel asked.

"I don't think you need to ask, Les; you know that you blagged it in, even when the man said he wasn't interested."

"Not true, not true; you know what they are like," Wurzel whinged with a nasal whine. This was his "Well, I know I fucked it up, but I'm not admitting to it" voice.

Wurzel blamed everything on everyone else but himself; oh, the strain of being a Supreme Being.

"Kevin, Kevin, Kevin," came the smarmy Cumbrian/Geordie brogue of Big Jim Rowan, Seven Bellies himself.

He had a dual accent as he was born in Tyneside (Geordie heaven) but moved to Cumbria six years ago and had picked up a bit of an accent, as you do when you live in a place long enough.

Totally flustered, Wurzel started stuttering, "Oh, oh, s-s-sorry JR; see you, Kev," and put the extension down.

"JR" was Wurzel's nickname for Jim Rowan, as he likened himself to JR Ewing out of *Dallas*, rich successful businessman, which he was not. Wurzel was terrified of JR (we'll call him that now, as you all know its Seven Bellies, anyway). Me, scared? Not likely; the sanctimonious bastard got on my tits (Geordie for "annoying"), and he knew it, but I'm very good at my job and he knows it; cor, what a hero.

"What you twining [Cumbrian for "moaning"] about now, Kevin?" JR asked in an exasperating manner.

"Nothing, Jim; just another one of Les's bad leads. The guy didn't want to know, and Les just blagged it in: 'Mr D'Arcy's passing anyway, so it's no problem for him to pop in and have an informal chat' syndrome." Sarcasm oozed from my voice. I couldn't help it.

"So what happened at your twelve o'clock?" JR spat out.

"Double ad, six hundred pounds cash," I spat back.

"Marvellous, marvellous." This was JR's happy voice now, and I could almost see his gigantic underpants filling with orgasmic rapture.

"You fucking changed your tune quick enough," I said to myself under my breath.

"Right, just get to your next client; three o'clock isn't it? Speak to you later, and Kevin, ring me," boomed the voice of JR. Click, end of conversation.

I was dismissed. *Oh well*, I thought, *who gives a fuck?* "Eat my shit and die, dickhead," I muttered under my breath.

My target figure for the week was ten sales; this would bring JR two thousand pounds profit and five hundred pounds for me. Luckily, being self-employed, I averaged twenty sales a week, a thousand pounds. JR netted about ten thousand pounds, plus all the perks (company house, cars, etc.), so all in all, it was a lucrative little business for one of us. Except Wurzel, he was crap at his job.

The three o'clock appointment was in Wilton, about fifteen miles from Larkhill. He was a glazier selling UPVC double glazing and wood frame glazing. I looked at the phone number and dialled it. Double glaziers are notorious for bombing out (cancelling appointments) or not turning up at all. Since I had to pay for my own petrol and other expenses, it was cheaper to make a quick phone call to confirm the appointment instead of wasting time, petrol, and wear and tear on TBWSB. Bleep, bleep, bleep, bleep went the phone. A rich melodious Brummy (Birmingham) accent answered.

"Hello, Monument Glaziers, Benny Santini speaking, how may I help you?

"Hello, Mr Santini, Kevin D'Arcy from *Workforce.* I am just ringing to confirm my three o'clock appointment." My watch said 1.48.

"Oh, I'm glad you rang me; your mate didn't leave me a contact number [Les's other favourite trick so they couldn't ring up and cancel]. Never mind," he continued. *Here we go again*, I thought. "I've got to go out now, but I'll be back at four o'clock, if you can make it then."

Thank God for small mercies; as it happens, my 4.30 appointment had been scratched out, so Mr Santini was my last one for the day. He was obviously an outsider; I worked that out because of the Brummy accent (clever shite, aren't I?), so maybe I was in with a chance. I had a knowing feeling in my gut I was going to do well here with the outsiders, but not the locals. Anyway, double glaziers usually took big ads, full pages, which meant more money.

"No problem at all, Mr Santini. Four o'clock is fine, but can I give you my mobile number, just in case? I know business is business, and you might have a big client or job."

"Great, Geordie, great," he said excitably. "Hold on, and I'll get a pen. Fire away, Geordie."

"My name is Kevin, by the way," I said. I hate it when they call you "Geordie" when you're from Newcastle or "Daff" from Wales or "Paddy" from Ireland, don't you?

"Okay, Geordie, okay, fire away."

Totally oblivious to my previous remark, I thought. Fuck it; the customer is always right, so JR says, and I rattled off my mobile phone number.

"Four o'clock, Geordie, four o'clock. Got the number, just in case. Ta ta for a bit" ("Bye" in Brummy).

The phone went down. I had two hours to kill. I shouldn't have used that last word, as it nearly came true.

Back to the hotel for a coffee. It's only a fifteen-minute drive from Larkhill, so I decided to have an hour's rest. I looked at the map: down the A360, turn left onto the A303, right onto Stonehenge Road, and back in Amesbury and the George Hotel; bliss.

"Black Dog" by Chris Rea off *God's Great Banana Skins* started playing. I noticed Stonehenge on my right as I cruised down the road; it looked different from this angle. With it being October, it was starting to get darker earlier, as it does in winter. "No one knows that Black Dog, I said no one knows that Black Dog, I said no one knows that Black Dog better than I," sang Chris, and then like something out of *Hellraiser*, the bastard appeared. As if by autosuggestion from the lyrics of the song, there stood a huge black dog.

Now, this son of a bitch was like the werewolf out of the film *American Werewolf in London*. You know the bit, when the young lad changed into the monster. It stood about three and a half feet high and was as long as it was broad. Its eyes were like two red rubies glistening in its huge, shaggy head. Its huge mouth hung open, showing you its fangs, and its long tongue lolled to one side, dripping saliva.

It was about forty yards ahead of me, standing motionless. As it happens, I was sticking to the speed limit of 30 mph; otherwise, I would have ploughed into it.

Christ, that would have made a mess of my Baby (my pet name for TBSWB) if I had hit it. I gently braked (the brakes are ABS, so you could nearly stop on a pound coin) and changed down the gears, fourth to third to second, then stopped and went into neutral, with the handbrake on. My hackles rose, and I visibly shuddered. This wasn't just getting whacked; this was fear. TBWSB gently ticked over, almost silently. We stared at each other, but surely it couldn't see me through the deep tinted windows. I felt it sensed me more than saw me.

It moved forward very slowly, very deliberately, towards me and the car. One of the first things that crossed my mind was, what if it jumped on my Baby? Its sheer size and weight would probably buckle the front spoiler and spotlights, dent the front bonnet and the turbo air vents, smash the heated front windscreen, and scratch the whole lot to bits with those huge paws and claws. Now, I'm not one to back down; I don't scare easily, but the facts and figures went through my mind like hypo-drive on a computer. It would cause at least five thousand pounds' worth of damage, I'd be off the road, which would result in loss of earnings, and waiting for new parts to be ordered would just draw things out even longer. This was deep shit, and no mangy flea-bitten werewolf lookalike was worth it.

I switched off the CD and turned a dial on the dashboard, which dimmed all the fascia lights; only a very low dim light remained, just enough to see all the dials, speedo, and fuel gauge. Not that I needed to see them because I knew this Baby like the back of my hand.

Whenever I got in the driving seat, switched on the ignition, and put her into gear, we became one, like lovers. I slipped the gears into reverse and released the handbrake. As I did, I patted the dashboard (I did this quite often as a form of endearment) and said to TBWSB, "Well now, Baby, let's see what we can do."

I slowly released the clutch and gently pressed down the accelerator. Smoothly and almost silently, we moved; all you could hear was the slight sound of gravel crunching under the tyres. The speedo hovered between 5 and 10 mph; the beast started moving at the same rate. Five yards, ten yards, fifteen yards we covered, and I kept looking in the rearview mirror to see if anything was coming. The road was clear but getting darker.

On and on, the beast plodded towards us, slowly building momentum. A lightbulb went on in my head; I had an idea. The beast and I were on the left-hand side of the road, and the right was clear. I slipped the car into neutral, and she kept on rolling backwards. I glanced forward, and the beast was increasing its speed. I judged it was going to pounce. I stepped on the clutch and put the car into first gear, ready for action. I quickly looked round from side to side, back to front; the road was clear. The beast was running now like an Olympic long jumper, striding with its long legs building up for its takeoff right onto my car, and if that happened, it would go straight through the windscreen. There would be no more me if it made contact.

It started to leap. I turned on the twin sets of headlamps and the two spot lamps in the front spoiler. With that lot on full beam, it was like looking at the sun. The beast's large ruby eyes shone like red hot coals; because of the intense light, it had to move its head to one side, as it was temporarily blinded.

"Too late, you bastard," I shouted as it had already started to jump and was in mid-flight.

As it started to take off, I popped the clutch and put my boot down on the accelerator. Her steel-belted radials gripped as I went from reverse to forward. The tyres spun and she burned rubber as she sped forward. The revs screamed up as I took off, veering to the right-hand side of the road. Her power-assisted steering is so sensitive; I can almost steer with one finger. Within seconds, the car was doing 50 mph. I put it straight into second gear, steering with my right hand, and the car was away in seconds. I glanced in the mirror; the wisps of smoke started to disappear, and I saw the beast, paws flailing amid the black skid marks the tyres had left on the ground. I could almost hear the crunch as it hit the ground, front paws down and tumbling over and over as it made contact with the ground. I throttled down, as we were doing over 80 mph; I shifted into fourth, the revs dropped, and we went to a steady 60 mph. I smiled and lifted my right middle finger and laughed, saying, "Twirl on that, you bastard."

I looked at my watch: 14.38 and 12 seconds. I was dying to get back to the hotel; sod the coffee, double Jack Daniels, crushed ice, a slice of lemon, and a drop of lemonade was what I needed to calm the old nerves down. The mobile started ringing. *Shit timing*, I thought.

"Hello, Kev D'Arcy; can I help you?"

"Hiya Geordie, Benny Santini, still with the client, so won't be able to make it, so I thought I'd give you a ring."

As I was tired and shaken, I was glad.

"No problem, Mr Santini; I'll get the office to ring and reappoint you another day. Bye now; thanks for ringing."

As that was my last appointment, I switched off my business mode and started to relax. I decided to send JR a fax when I got back to the hotel to let him know what happened. Now I was ready to get pissed and hopefully see what's in Shelta's knickers.

Chapter 6

Fun at the Hotel

It was 15:10 and 6 seconds when I pulled into the hotel car park. I stopped and switched off the ignition partway, so the power was still coming through for the machines. I wrote a fax message explaining what happened with Mr Santini and asked them to rebook him in my next day's appointments. I pressed the autodial, and the paper started feeding through the machine. Five minutes later, a fax with my appointments came back. As it started to come through, I gave it a cursory glance: Nothing at 9 a.m.; 10:30 a.m. appeared, and there was writing next to the time. I didn't bother looking at the name or the full address; I only wanted to know the area. Amesbury hit me in the eyes as I scanned the sheet. Magic, I thought, no travelling. I may as well look at the name and full address. What I saw was like a blow to my face: Mr Toutaitis de la Wyle, The Abbey, Amesbury Park, Amesbury.

This should be interesting. I wondered what business he had, apart from the hotel. The trade Wurzel had put down was wrought iron works; that accounted for his strange hands, I thought. "Oh, well, a nice lie-in in the morning," I said to myself. I can see the abbey from my bedroom window, and it was no more than five minutes away from the hotel. I noticed some more names and addresses appearing and then a load of writing I recognised as JR's spidery scrawl straight away. Fuck this for a game of soldiers; I sighed, as I knew he'd be moaning again.

"I'm finished for the day, fat man," I shouted at the machine, as though it was Jim Rowan himself. I switched off the ignition, turned off all the machines, punched in the code for the alarm, set the immobiliser, and switched on the talking alarm. "Please do not touch this car; I am fully alarmed" came out in TBWSB's robotic female voice. The Chubb key fitted snugly in the lock as I turned it. The sharp resonating click of the central locking echoed round the empty car park. As I started walking towards the hotel entrance, I ran my hand across the roof and down the bodywork of the car, stroking it like a large cat. When I reached the back spoiler, I patted it. "Goodnight, Baby," I crooned like a master to its animal, God, I love that car.

The back door of the hotel opened, and Shelta appeared. To say she was wearing a skirt would have been an understatement, as it was more like a leather belt. There's an expression on Tyneside (Geordie land): "She's got legs that go all the way up to her bum." These didn't; they practically reached her ears. She had one of those small halter tops on, you know the ones that look like a bra, and her nipples stuck out like two dustbins on a hill. Her curly platinum hair blew back in the wind, and her gorgeous green eyes were smiling and laughing. The old trouser snake in my underpants stirred as I looked at her nipples pushing through the fabric, as she wasn't wearing a bra. As she sashayed towards me, she could see I was looking at her breasts and nipples. She gave me a sultry look, and as she walked, she arched her back slightly, making them jut out further. Her miniskirt rose up slightly when she did this. *Ya dorty bitch* ("You dirty bitch" in Geordie), my mind screamed because as she did this, her skirt rose up slightly, and I could see a mound of platinum blonde hair poking out. She wasn't wearing any knickers. As I put my eyes back in their sockets, I looked straight at her nipples again and asked, "Is it cold out here, or are you just glad to see me?"

She looked at my open jacket to the front of my trousers bulging away, as the trouser snake had risen to its full height and was nearly popping out the top of my pants. Quick as a whip, she retorted, "I bet you were the only lad at school that won the three-legged race on his own."

Smart as well as beautiful, I thought.

“Love the car,” she said as she walked up beside me. “I came to see what that strange talking noise was that I just head.”

“That’s my Baby,” I said, pointing to TBWSB.

“You know what they say about men with big cars,” she said, smiling at the front of my pants again.

The way my prick was throbbing, I thought the one-eyed milkman (another Geordie term for prick) was going to deliver any second now. Before I knew what happened, she set her perfectly rounded bum on the bonnet, and TBWSB went straight into action. All hell broke loose. The lights started flashing, the sirens went off, the number plate clicked open and started flashing “I have been stolen,” and a male robot voice shouted, “I am being stolen; call the police.” The female robotic voice cried, “Please do not touch this car; I am fully alarmed.” Boy, was there a racket.

Shelta jumped about six feet into the air and then slid down the bonnet with her legs upended. She sat there, skirt up her back and her legs splayed apart. I wanted to find out what was in her knickers; now I knew. I had a remote control for TBWSB which shut the whole system down at the press of a button. I pressed it immediately, and the whole system deactivated. I couldn’t help laughing at Shelta, lying there as she looked like a dead sparrow with her legs in the air.

“What in God’s name was all that?” she asked.

“Well,” I answered, “like all ladies, the Big White Super Bitch [I used her full name] doesn’t like being touched unless she wants to, only she has a different way of showing it.”

I held out my hands to her to help her up, as she sat there trying to regain her composure. She grabbed my hands as I helped lift her up. I could still see right up her skirt, and she knew it; she smiled as she got to her feet.

“Like what you see?” she asked.

Why not test the water? I thought, as I replied, “Well, I’ve had nothing to eat all day, and I quite fancy some scampi. That golden brown outside with lovely pink meat inside just melts in my mouth.”

She grasped the analogy of her tadger (Geordie for “vagina”) straight away and smiled, then she pouted and replied, “Well, we’ll just see what we can do about that, then.” As we walked to the hotel, I pressed the remote control for the alarm and reset all the systems on TBWSB. “Do not touch me; I am fully alarmed” started sounding as the system went through its activation procedure, and I heard the bleep bleep, in the background as we closed the door to the hotel entrance.

“Some car,” Shelta said.

“Some lady,” I replied, smiling cheekily back at her; her eyes twinkled back at me, and her body seemed to ooze lust and sexuality. *Sod the chips*, I thought, *scampi will do just nicely,* as a vision of what was under her skirt came to my mind.

As if she had read my mind, Shelta turned and said, “If you’d like to go to the bar and order the drinks, I’ll start preparing your dinner.”

I understood the innuendo immediately and said, “I’ll get two Jack Daniels, crushed ice, slice of lemon, and a drop of lemonade, if that suits you.”

“That’ll do nicely; see you in fifteen minutes.”

“I think I’ve died and gone to heaven,” I whistled as I entered the bar.

“Good evening, Mr D’Arcy; had a good day?” asked the rich baritone voice of Tony de la Wyle. His head appeared over the cocktail bar as I turned to see where the voice was coming from. So he works here as well.

“Two triple Jack Daniels, please,” I asked politely, explaining, “and could you put a slice of lemon in first, crushed ice on top, then the Jack Daniels, then the same amount of lemonade on top?”

“Oh, a man who likes his drink,” Tony quipped.

“All Geordies like their drink, as you’ll find out later on,” I jibed back at him.

I put my briefcase on the table and sat down. I opened up the case, took out my diary, and looked at the next day’s business: Tuesday 4 October, 10.30 a.m., Toutaitis de la Wyle, nothing for twelve noon, 1.30 p.m. Fiona Leeming, 29 Carlton Court, Middle Wallop, telephone number, and it said for occupation, Business Consultant. After that, no more appointments.

Wurzel must be struggling I thought. A large pair of hands banged down the drinks on the table, and I jumped slightly, as I was lost in my thoughts, working out how far Middle Wallop was from Amesbury.

“Your drinks, sir.” Tony emphasised the “sir” in a sanctimonious way. “Shall I charge them to your room?”

“That’ll do nicely, waiter,” I jeered back as he handed me the receipt to sign.

I noticed his hands looked red, raw, and sore. “No one knows that Black Dog, I said no one knows that Back Dog better than I” resounded in my ears as I got whacked with a vengeance. His black eyes narrowed as he looked straight at me; was it another trick of the light, or was there a small pinpoint of red light there? I went to get the receipt and deliberately touched his hand with mine, as my psychic powers kicked in automatically. He flinched like it was like a massive dose of static electricity coursing through him. *Bad dog*, I thought, as the red light disappeared in his eyes. I signed the receipt and handed it back to him; he warily took it from my hand.

That'll teach you, you bastard, I thought as he turned and walked back to the bar, muttering what sounded like some Latin dialect. *Get down, Shep; get down*, I laughed to myself as the Jack Daniels slid down my throat like mother's milk. I lit a cigarette and inhaled the smoke deep in my lungs to get the nicotine's full effect. As I blew the smoke back out, I saw a ghostly figure appear through the haze. Now to say Shelta looked stunning was another understatement. She stood tall and proud, and her long blonde hair was a mass of curls and ringlets. Her green eyes shone, and her lips were glossed ruby red. She wore a long satin dress the same colour as her lipstick; the cut was very low, and her breasts swelled like two small melons. As she walked towards me, I could see the dress was split right up the right leg, showing off her magnificent thigh.

"Dinner is served, sir," she said, giggling, "but I hope you can supply the tartare sauce."

A vision of her lovely golden mound with the pink lips sticking out, covered in spunk, appeared in my mind. The simile of the scampi, cut in two with the pink flesh jutting out, oozing with tartare sauce, was effective.

"Screw the food," I punned, laughing, "But what's for afters?"

"Wait and see," she returned, pouting and posing like a low-budget porn film.

As she sat down beside me, her dress gaped, exposing her beautiful thigh, and her scent drifted round with a heady aroma.

She sipped her Jack Daniels and said, "It's very strong but nice, just like you."

I'm in or not (Geordie for scoring with a woman), I thought, *she's giving it to me on a plate* (another pun).

We laughed and joked for two hours; I told her about where I lived and my wonderful family, as her uncle glared ominously at us from behind the bar. We had five Jack Daniels each and were getting rather tipsy, as you do.

"Alright, boyo," boomed a voice across the bar, and in strode Graham Hood, grinning broadly. "Whatever that is, I'll have one," he said. "It's obviously working for you two."

"Waiter [*Here boy*, I laughed to myself], three more of these, and make it quick," I shouted in my best Geordie voice in mocking tones to Tony de la Wyle behind the bar.

His face was a picture as he was so angry he was nearly spitting blood and was it the drink getting to me, or was his face in the shadows taking on a dog like appearance, red eyes glaring.

Shelta must have sensed this and as she stood up, she said, "I'll get these ones; you've spent enough already," and walked towards her uncle as Graham was rambling away about something.

I wasn't really taking any notice, I glanced over at Shelta and her uncle. They seemed to be arguing, about me probably. *Fuck you, Tony*, I though; *the customer is always right*. JR's words sprang to mind.

She glided back to the table with a tray full of drinks and also some bar snacks. "There we are, boys," she said as she put the drinks, three Jack Daniels, two pints of bitter, half a pint of lager, and a selection of nuts, cheese, and biscuits on the table. "I thought you might like something long and cool with your snacks."

"I could just do with a pint," I said. "You must be a mind reader."

"Not had your dinner yet?" Graham asked, and Shelta and I looked into each other's eyes and burst out laughing. "Have I missed something?" he asked, puzzled.

"No, private joke," I said, smiling lustfully back at Shelta.

The little elfin girl from the burger van came in as we were nibbling at our snacks and sipping our drinks. She walked over to the bar, and Tony opened the counter and let her through. He muttered a few words to her and walked towards the reception.

"Goodnight, Mr de la Wyle," I said as he walked past our table. "See you 10.30 a.m. tomorrow, sharp."

His eyes spat venom as he glared at me. He flicked his head forward, strode forcefully towards the door, and banged it open, nearly taking it off its hinges.

"Someone's in a bad mood," Graham said, and as I looked towards Shelta, she had a worried look on her face.

She quietly stared at me with those big green eyes and said, "He's a bad man to cross, Kev; be careful."

"Geordies don't scare easily," I quipped back.

But if that was him in the shape of the dog today (I shuddered), he had scared me then. I had a feeling I had pushed things a bit too far. *Can't the man have a laugh?* I wondered. Obviously not, and a strange feeling of disaster swept over me. *Fuck it,* I thought as I swallowed my pint. *You're only thirty-nine years old once.*

The three of us laughed and joked and told stories, and when I looked at my watch, it said 23:15. "My, doesn't time fly when you're enjoying yourself?" I asked, looking at Graham.

He smiled back with a lopsided grin as the Jack Daniels and pints had taken their affect.

"I think I'm getting the eye," Graham replied, looking over at the bar, grinning like the Cheshire Cat. Both Shelta and I looked over and saw the burger girl smiling back at us.

"That's my cousin Justine," slurred Shelta as she downed her ninth Jack Daniels.

Please don't flake out [fall asleep] *on me*, my mind said rapidly. *I haven't had my dinner yet.*

She smiled back wistfully and shouted, "Come over here, Justine, and get yourself a drink on the house, since your dad is gone."

Dad, I thought. *Tony de la Wyle's her dad; better watch myself.*

Shelta made the introductions; we shook hands, and as she sat down next to Graham, his smile widened. We drank and talked for a while, and when I looked round, I realised we were the only people left in the bar. By now, the drink was getting to me, and I knew I'd had enough. Even after the bits of cheese and biscuits, I was still hungry. *Screw the food,* I said to myself, and a vision of golden and pink scampi covered in tartare sauce came to me again.

Shelta smiled at me wickedly.

"Well, ladies and gents," I said, "it's getting a bit late, and I have a long day tomorrow. I'm going to have a bit of supper in my room, if that is alright with you, Shelta, then off to sleep. Thank you for your company; I really enjoyed it."

"Well, I'll go and prepare your supper while you say goodnight, and I'll bring it to your room," Shelta said as she glided across the floor towards the stairs.

“Well, goodnight again, you two,” I said to Graham and Justine, but they were lost in each other, giggling away. God, don’t you just love room service? I smiled to myself as I walked up the stairs to my room, prick throbbing at the thought of all that lovely scampi.

Chapter 7

"When You Really Love a Woman"

When I reached the top of the stairs, I saw the light under my door. Ah, dinner is served. I pushed the door open, and there she was, laying on the double bed next to the window. The curtains were open, and the pale moonlight shone on her hair, which made it shimmer like a platinum halo. Her gorgeous naked body was stretched out on the bed, her knees were up, and her legs stretched wide part. There's the scampi; now here comes the tartare sauce. My one-eyed milkman was throbbing and ready to make its delivery. As I undressed and took off my underpants, my prick was bursting out of them like a cobra ready to strike.

"Big car, big dick?" Shelta asked, grinning as she looked at my prick.

As I looked between her legs, the golden curls and pink petals of her tadger glistened as she grew wet with anticipation.

Now as you've already gathered, I love music. I also love to make love to music. I picked up one of the tapes I carry with me to relax to. It was *The Private Music of Tangerine Dream*, all electronic and very moody. As I switched the music on, I slipped beside Shelta on the bed, and that sweet musky smell of her sex wafted around the room. Now, I am a very attentive lover and very gentle with women. I am not a "wham, bam, and thank you, ma'am" type of guy. I cater to a woman's needs. I love to explore a woman's body and for her to explore mine, so we can find each other's needs. She grabbed for me, and I gently put my finger on her lips as if to say shush. I caressed her hair with my hands and then kissed her forehead. I gently stroked her body with the fingers of my right hand, moving it from side to side and up and down, feeling the smooth contours of her skin. I cocked my leg over her, straddled her body, and gently pressed my hands in hers, moving them back over her head. My lips gently kissed both her eyes, left then right. And as I kissed the tip of her nose, I felt her body tremble. Those luscious ruby lips pouted as I gave her a long, passionate kiss. I placed my hands round her head and stroked her ears and licked her neck and shoulders. Her head was back, and her eyes glittered as she made little gasping sighs with her breath. My hands stroked down her neck and shoulders as I bent towards her breasts. They were firm and full, and her nipples stood erect. I gently licked the end of the right one and then sucked the full top of it, nipple and all. I ran my tongue over the whole breast and down into the ridge in between and up to the left breast and did the same with it, licking and sucking her stiff nipple.

I could feel her legs spread wider as I eased my way down her body; my prick, hard and throbbing, rubbed against her as I descended. Shelta arched her back, and I felt her golden mound thrust up, so I grabbed a pillow and put it under her bum for support. Our eyes met; she had a glazed look as she licked her lips. Her breathing was laboured as I started kissing the hollow of her stomach and flicked my tongue in and around her belly button. I reached down and touched the underneath of her right calf as I moved my lips and tongue across the bottom of her stomach; my chin could feel her lovely curly mound brushing against it. My fingers gently traced their way up the inside of her thigh, just touching the outside of her fleshy vaginal lips. Her back arched even further as my head was sliding down to her hairy hole of delight. She grabbed my hair as I moved my hand over the top of her thigh and underneath to probe and stroke the cheeks of her firm bum.

“Three Bikes in the Sky,” track 7 on the tape, floated eerily round the room. I could smell the sweet musk smell of her sex as my tongue slid across her wiry pubic hair and touched her clitoris, which was sticking out hard and round. She gasped loudly as my finger slid up the crease of her bum to her wet tadger. She tugged at my hair, and I thought *Bloody hell, there isn’t that much; be careful*, as my bald bit reflected in the moonlight. I lifted my head and stretched forward to kiss her. Her lips hungrily met mine, and our two tongues entwined like serpents fighting. The rose petal lips of her tadger parted and devoured my middle finger as I slowly inserted it into her tight, dripping hole. Shelta bit my tongue gently and her head rocked from side to side as I probed deeper. The warm flesh of her insides squelched and grew wetter as I waggled my finger up and down.

The lips of her tadger spread apart as I slowly removed my finger. We kissed hungrily, and she grabbed for my prick with her right hand and grasped it. It gave one almighty throb as she did this and seemed to stiffen more. My middle and third finger gently massaged her clitoris, and the lips parted again as I moved my fingers downward. The elastic fleshy sides spread and gripped my two fingers as I slid them in and out. She became wetter and wetter as I moved them up and down her clitoris and inside her hair hole of delight. She started masturbating my prick as the pace increased faster and faster. Now, you might wonder if I have brewer's droop (too much alcohol so you can't perform). Well, I suffer the reverse; by some strange quirk of fate, my prick gets harder and harder and will not go down, especially if he is enjoying himself; he seems to have a mind of his own. Darn clever, these trouser snakes. My fingers moved faster and faster, and Shelta squealed louder and started dribbling as her orgasm started. I could feel we were both ready to come, so I removed my fingers with a plop and laid my hand to rest on her arm for her to stop also.

Melodious little sounds, like gasps, escaped from her mouth. I looked at her angelic face, her great big beautiful eyes as wide as saucers sparkled back. A line from Bryan Adams's song, "When You Really Love a Woman," came flooding into my brain and made my heart lurch. "When you can see your unborn children in her eyes" echoed round my insides. *God*, I thought, *I think I'm in love, and I don't really know her.* My heart flipped.

Shelta wrapped her legs around me, and I could feel her protruding mound, hot, wet, and hairy, press against my groin. Time to put the tartare sauce on the scampi. As I slid into her slice of heaven, her back arched, and I thrust forward at the same time. She was so wet by now, I slid in with ease. I felt her love lips grasp round the shaft and her hole tighten as I slid into her. The whole length of my prick stroked her hard, round clitoris as it entered her. She squealed with delight and raked her long talons against my back and dug them in. I had a feeling she would be a scratcher and moaner; I knew the signs. My ex-lover Sharon (Slut Bag, I called her) was exactly the same; more about her later.

Synchronicity is the only word I can use; it was perfection. We were like two sexual alchemists; the chemistry was perfect, and as track 9, "Electric Lion," synthesised its way out, I thought it very apt, as her pussy was electrifying. I knew this track like the back of my hand; it's perfect to make love to. Eight minutes and thirteen seconds of musical bliss; I knew I had to come at the end of it, as I could hold back no longer. Flesh met flesh; pelvic bone and pelvic bone thrashed at each other in a sexual fury. Shelta stopped and started to push my chest backwards with her hands. *Shit, what's happening?* I thought as she pushed me further backward, and I slid out of her. She twirled me round, put me on my back, and then straddled me.

"My turn," she said breathlessly. "You've been in charge long enough; let me show you a few tricks now."

My trouser snake stood there, tall and proud, as she pulled back her flaps and eased her way onto my slippery shaft. She slid slowly down, thrust back up, and arched her breasts; her nipples were jutting out, pointing to the moon. She put her hands behind her neck and started gyrating her hips. She had become one with the beat of the music and was dancing on my prick; it felt as though it was in a meat mincer. The music rose to a crescendo. I gently squeezed her nipples, and she gyrated faster and faster, using my prick like a corkscrew. She tossed back her hair as she started to lift up her arms towards the ceiling; we could both feel ourselves in perfect timing; we had become one with each other, a single sexual entity, starting to head towards an explosive orgasm. (One thing that went through my mind was Geordie girls say, "I'm coming, I'm coming." Shelta was so posh, she would say, "I'm arriving, I'm arriving.")

Then the most amazing thing happened: She bent back her head so her long hair cascaded down around us, moaned slightly as her body shuddered, and spread her arms upwards, palms and fingers spread wide, pointing towards the heavens. In between her fingers, a blue light appeared. It started to twirl round and round, growing bigger and burning a deep electric blue; well, I'll go to Whitley Bay and say she was forming a matrix. As my groin rumbled, deep down, I felt the spunk rising; thar she blows!

I glanced at the mirror on the dressing table, and in the reflection, I could see Stonehenge in the distance, pulsating with a deep red glow. As if by command, she plunged her long fingers into the matrix, and the red glow seemed to shoot from Stonehenge and reflect off the mirror into the room. It was like a scene in *The Exorcist,* as the room was bathed in a blood red light. Track 9 on the tape seemed to be in perfect harmony with the light, like some kind of cosmic disco.

She began breathing faster and faster, and as I felt our juices bursting forward in orgasmic delight, the colours merged like a sexual frenzy. The electric blue matrix was swirling round her arms and head as her fingers seemed to plunge deeper and deeper. Deep gold flecks appeared in the red light, lights like you see on a disco wall, flashing round and round. She gazed down at me, eyes glowing green but with that lovely dreamy quality you get during sex. Her hands arced down, slowly bringing the blue light towards me. The timer on the tape said eight minutes of the music had lapsed as she started her downward descent. I guessed she wanted to form a matrix with my hands. Eight minutes, five seconds, six seconds, seven seconds; she grew nearer. At eight minutes, thirteen seconds, exactly as the music stopped, our hands met. In the film *Cocoon*, an alien girl makes love with a human

man. They use their hands to make love, and when their hands meet, a blinding ball of light appears. Well, this was much the same. As our fingertips touched and then the palms, it was as though the cosmos was a transistor, and we were the batteries; put the two together, and we were creating galactic music. We hadn't made the earth move, like most lovers; we had literally moved the heavens. Time seemed to stand still as we bathed in the now-whitish electric blue light.

We came at the same time; undulating waves of euphoria swept through us both, wave after wave of sheer ecstasy. As our waves of pleasure subsided, so did the lights, slowing down as our bodies did, everything going back to normal.

I breathed a great long sigh and said, "That's the best scampi and tartare sauce I've ever had. What's for afters?"

"Now don't be greedy," she replied. "How about some pussy pie for you, and I'll have dick on a stick?"

She smiled impishly, twisting round into the 69 position and shoving her beautiful tadger, all covered in our orgasmic juices, into my face.

"Oh, pussy pie with cream," I said, starting to lick her out.

"Dick on a stick with creamy filling," she said as she licked up and down my shaft.

After we finished tasting each other, we lay back on the bed, shattered.

"My compliments to the chef, but I don't think JR would appreciate this on the bill," I joked.

"Bar snack, scampi in a basket, with a sweet," she said as she snuggled in drowsily.

As I cradled her head in my shoulder, she cocked her leg over my thigh; I could feel her warm, damp tadger sticking to it like a limpet on a rock as we both dozed off to sleep.

Just before I fell asleep, my eyes caught the reflection of Stonehenge in the mirror again. It was still glowing red, I thought, as I drifted into a happy oblivion, my new love beside me.

Chapter 8

Second Day on the Road

At 7 a.m., the alarm buzzed, and I returned to the living. Shelta's long golden tresses were spread across the pillows like a blanket, and her eyes snapped awake. The sun shone through the window and hit her eyes; they glowed green like a cat's. She smiled a smile of warm contentment.

"Hiya beautiful," I said, smiling back.

"Morning, handsome," she replied.

I went to kiss her; pooh: dragon breath (bad breath the morning after).

"I think we'd better clean our teeth first," I said. "I've got a mouth like the bottom of a budgie's bird cage.

"You're right," she said. "Mine doesn't feel too good, either."

I handed her some mouthwash after I sipped some myself and rinsed it round my mouth. She took some and did the same.

"That's better; now, give us a kiss," I said in my best Geordie accent as I grabbed her and pulled her close to me.

As our lips met, I could feel her nipples against my chest and then the full roundness of her breasts flattens on mine. She thrust her hips against mine, and I felt her lovely hairy mound, soft and wet, against my rising prick. I ran my right hand down her back and across her bum, easing my fingers round and grabbing her crotch from behind. As my right middle finger flicked her love petals open and slipped into her wet hole, my prick stiffened like a rod of iron against her belly.

"Sausage for breakfast, I take it," she said.

"Makes a change from spirits," I replied, making reference to yesterday morning. "And we need to talk later."

"Later, but not now. I see you like it from behind," she said, referring to my fingers gently massaging her tadger from the back.

"Sausage [prick] and kipper [vagina] for breakfast it is, then," I said, laughing as I turned her round and bent her over.

She spread her legs and leaned against the dressing table to support herself, smiling at me in the mirror. My prick slipped inside her, and her bum rose as her back arched. She groaned as I placed my hands on her hips.

"Breakfast is now being served," she gasped as I pumped into her, flesh slapping against flesh.

We both came in minutes. After we finished and she stood back up, my spunk started dribbling down her legs, mixed with light splatters of blood. She looked down in amazement at the pink coloured flow dribbling down her legs.

"My God," she said, "that's the first time in three years this has happened; now we really do need to talk."

"How 'bout after a shower?" I asked, opening the windows and putting a tape in the machine.

"That would be lovely," she replied as Michael Bolton's dulcet tones sang "You Send Me."

I love music first thing in the morning, and this song reminded me of what I thought about Shelta last night. We got into the shower together; as we washed and soaped each other, I sang, "Darling you send me, I know you send me. Darling you send me, honest you do, honest you do. Lover, you thrill me, I know you thrill me, Oh you thrill me, honest you do, honest you do," in harmony with Michael (or so I thought).

We dried off, and I watched her dress; she was so feminine, and I thought the words of the song playing suited my feelings towards her perfectly.

"I must rush," she said, running towards the door. "My mum will be coming on duty soon, and if she sees me like this, I'll get called all the sluts under the sun, which I am, but I don't want her to know it."

God, I love it when a woman talks dirty, don't you?

I put out my double breasted grey/blue suit, pale blue shirt, dark blue tie and handkerchief set and black alligator shoes and then went through my usual rigmarole of getting dressed. I had a quick shave with the electric razor and picked up all my gear and went down stairs for breakfast.

As I entered the reception, Shelta's mum called out, "Morning, Mr D'Arcy."

"Morning, Mrs De'Danann, but please call me Kev," I said.

"Only if you call me Iuatha," she replied.

"That's fine by me," I said, looking at her thinking how unlike her brother she was. Him slim, dark, and moody, and her plump, blonde, and jolly. *Funny old world, isn't it?* I thought, wondering if her husband, Shelta's dad, was around.

"What would you like for breakfast, Kev?" Iuatha asked.

I thought back at what Shelta and I had just done and mused silently, *If you only knew, I've just had your daughter for breakfast.*

"Just coffee will do me fine, Iuatha."

"Sausages and kippers are nice," she replied, smirking.

Fuck me! Are they all psychic round here rattled in my brain as I headed towards the dining room. The coffee was perfect, hot and sweet. I pressed memory 1 on the mobile phone, and the Workforce telephone number appeared as it started dialling.

"Hello, *Workforce*, Supreme Being speaking."

Where is Seven Bellies? I thought as Wurzel's posh, la de dah voice rasped out of the handset.

"Morning, Wurzel," I said. "Where is Seven Bellies?"

"That's Mr Kent to you, oh balding one," replied Wurzel's sarcastic tone.

"When my hair gets as thin as your mouth is fat, then I'll start worrying, you subhuman, smelly-as-fuck pig," I quickly retorted. This could go on for hours, as we truly hated each other, so I said, "Les, this is costing 50p per minute, and since if wit was shit, you'd be constipated, there's no point carrying on with this idle banter, alright?"

Typical Wurzel; I know it's hard to function with only one brain cell.

"Ring me back, Les, and I'll fuck with your brain as much as you like, since you're paying," I said, cutting him off. Thirty seconds later, the phone rang. "Hello, Les."

"How did you know it was me?" muttered the Supreme Being, in all his wisdom.

"Well, if there was a tax on brains, you'd be in for a massive rebate," I sneered.

Iuatha was sitting next but one table away from me, laughing her head off, tears rolling down her cheeks, so I gave her my famous Burt Reynolds lookalike smile and winked at her; she laughed even harder. The whinging voice started again.

"Enough, Les, enough; unlike you, I have business to do, and so have you, judging by the amount of appointments in. So is fat man there?"

"He's out for the day," Wurzel whinged. "Big business meeting, very important."

Now this meant he was going on the piss (going to get drunk) and was going to play golf and act the big man (be arrogant) with other businessmen. Poor Wurzel was too naïve to realise this, as he was overawed by Seven Bellies. *Great, one day's reprieve*, I thought and then said, "Mr Santini needs reappointing, so I would give him a ring. Any more appointments in, as there are only two for today?"

"No, just the 10.30 a.m. and one o'clock," the Supreme Being answered.

"Okay, I'll ring you after the second one. Bye." I switched the phone off.

I turned towards Iuatha and asked, "Any chance of another coffee?"

"You can have as many as you want after that cabaret act," she said, still laughing, "Best laugh I've had in a while."

I thought back to Graham Hood; he had said the same. They don't have many laughs round here. *I'll have to change that,* I thought and smiled wickedly when Iuatha brought my coffee. I thanked her and looked at my watch: 9.07 and 16 seconds, it said. As Iuatha tidied up her cup and plate, I noticed nobody else had been in the dining room.

"Not many people come here at this time of the year," Iuatha said, answering my thoughts.

As she switched on the radio, Shelta came into mind, and I now knew who she had inherited her gift from. It was uncanny the way the two of them read my mind. As I was psychic too, I put it down to that. The weather report came over the radio.

"Salisbury and the surrounding districts will be stormy today," said the female voice. "Thunder and lighting and heavy rain is expected."

Just what I needed, crap weather. I hated driving in the rain, as did TBWSB. I sipped on my coffee and looked at the map. Turn right on to the High Street, onto Church Street, and just past Church Lane on the right was a road leading to the Abbey. Quarter of a mile, if that, I thought, five minutes in TBWSB. 9.40 And 8 seconds said my watch; I still had half an hour.

"Off to see my brother, then," remarked Iuatha.

"Yeah, 10.30," I replied.

"Be careful, Kev; he can be very intimidating," she said, concern showing on her face.

"You obviously didn't hear about our run-in last night, then?" I asked.

"No, I was out visiting my dead husband's grave on Vespasian's Camp." As if pre-empting my thoughts again, she added, "Lugus died on the first of November last year, on the Samhain, the festival of the dead. He had an accident." The tears that had been from laughter now turned to tears of pain. "Ex-excuse m-m-me," she said, stammering as she tried to stop herself from crying and ran into the kitchen.

So that is where her dad is, I thought; *dead and buried. Now I know.*

Lugus, Iuatha, and Shelta-Thari De'Danann; they were some exotic names for a family. When I speak to Shelta later, one of the questions I'll ask her was what nationality she was. 10.06 And 58 seconds appeared on the screen of my watch; I may as well make an early start. As I entered the car park, I could hear the distant rumble of thunder. Dark clouds rolled across the sky, giving the impression of the middle of the night. I pressed the remote control at TBWSB. She went through the process of disarming herself.

"Morning, Baby," I said as I unlocked the door and patted her roof fondly. I sat down, put my briefcase on the seat, and then set all the machines in motion. "All Right Now" by Tree (one of my all-time favourite bands) came blasting out of all four speakers as I switched on the ignition and pulled away. "All right now, baby, it is all right now, all right now baby, it is all right now," I sang with Paul Rodgers as the thunder exploded.

There was a sign for the abbey on the right after I went past Church Lane on the left. I turned right into the driveway, and the abbey loomed up, dark and satanic, in front of me. Lightning forked through the sky above it, reminding me of something out of a Hammer horror film. The sky turned red, and at the same time, "The Sky Is Burning" by Bad Company came on the radio. Yet another strange coincidence.

I pulled up to the front of the house and saw a sign which said "Tradesman's Entrance." That's me; I took it and drove up to the door. It started to rain; I looked around and there at the door stood a scowling Tony de la Wyle. He couldn't see me through the tinted windows, but I could see him. I could feel I was going to get blown away (knocked back on a sale). The rain came down hard and heavy, and by the time I reached the door, I was soaked.

“Good morning, Tony,” I said, trying to break the ice.

“Mr de la Wyle, if you don’t mind, Mr D’Arcy. I like to keep things formal when I talk business.”

As I extended my hand to shake his, I replied, “That’s fine by me, Mr de la Wyle. I agree with you entirely.”

His face broke into a smile, and he grabbed my hand and shook it (there was no silly tricks by either of us; it was a genuine, friendly handshake).

As he led us down to his office, he turned and said, “I think you and I are going to get on famously. I have something that will interest you immensely.”

Two huge Gothic-type doors stood before us; he pushed them open. A huge stone chamber stood before us, full of every weapon you could think of. Swords, muskets, maces, spears; you name it, he had it. One of my favourite martial arts is kendo, using Japanese swords called katanas; he had them all, and at a glance, some went back to the twelfth century. They were priceless. I stood, amazed and dumbfounded.

He grinned like a Cheshire Cat and offered, “Would you like to try one?

I was honoured. There was one which caught my eye. It was nearly four feet long in its black scabbard, which was ornately decorated with gold dragons and serpents. The handle had a beautiful carved gold and black shaft, which had a design like a family crest on it. I assumed it had belonged to an emperor or shogun (a military governor) or samurai warrior.

I switched onto what I call my kendo mode and took the priceless artefact off the wall. I took the sword out of its scabbard and twirled it round and round and up and down at lightning speed; the sword had become an extension of my body, as it is supposed to do. Now I'm not going to bore you with all the martial art terminology; I don't agree with it. If you've seen a martial arts film with them using katanas, it will help you form a picture. I finished the sequence and flashed the blade back into its scabbard in my left hand.

Just before the hilt hit the top, I put my left thumb up to the oncoming blade. *Why?* you ask. It is the code of practice in kendo that if you draw the blade, you must draw blood; if not someone else's, you must draw your own blood. The blade was honed to perfection, razor sharp, as it should be. Still fully tensed as the hilt hit home, eyes blazing, the blood spurting out of my thumb, I then switched off and relaxed and then bowed.

"Arigato gozaimasu" ("Thank you, sir" in Japanese).

Visibly astounded by what I had just done with the sword and had said to him, Tony then said, "I'm amazed, Mr D'Arcy. I had no idea you knew how to use such a weapon. May I beg your indulgence and have a practice with you?"

"I would be honoured," I replied, taking off my jacket.

We both unsheathed our swords and bowed to each other; the fight had begun.

Tony came straight at me, sword whirling like an aeroplane propeller. I could see now why he had such strong hands, as you needed a lot of strength to hold these swords. I stepped back sideways and with both hands swept the blade up towards his blade. It stopped like putting a stick in the spokes of a bicycle's wheel. As I caught up with the momentum, his sword flew out of his hand and landed point down in the floor, where it stood, shuddering. His eyes grew wide in surprise, and as he shook his head in amazement, I crouched slightly and raised my sword up and back, hilt behind my head and the blade facing perpendicular to the middle of his face.

"Your move," I said in a low, steady voice.

He walked over to his katana, pulled it out of the wooden floor, and said, "My, you are good, Mr D'Arcy," slashing quickly at my head as he spoke. Our swords echoed with a clang as they hit each other side to side, up and down, and back to front. After a couple minutes, we paused, taking each other's measure of skill. Tony glared at me, eyes black, and we took up the fighting stance again, swords up and back, facing each other. We clashed swords again, slashing at each other whilst twisting and turning at the same time. We aimed blows at every part of the body, trying to disable each other.

Shit, this guy is really serious, I thought as he rained down blows at me. These swords were made for cutting you to bits; they could make you into chopped liver in about three seconds. *Enough,* I thought, as I went into the same sequence as he had at the beginning, and my sword started swirling round. *But this time, I will show you how to do it properly*, I mused to myself. Tony watched, fascinated, as I went into my sequence. I had learned now not to underestimate him, and I knew he would try to stop me as I had him, but boy, was he in for a surprise. Now, with this type of sequence, you must totally concentrate because if you slip, you are dead or disabled.

As he watched in amazement through the whirring blade, I saw a blurred image of his face. As he went to strike, I saw his eyes gleam red, and I immediately tapped into the matrix. I tingled from head to toe, and as I did, I started to glow with a blue haze and felt Shelta's presence. Our matrixes had become one. He did as I had guessed and thrust his blade towards mine, but he cut down, not up, like I had. Mine had been a movement to disarm someone; his was a movement to disable someone and cause maximum damage. Pre-empting his move (knowing he was the type who played dirty to win) as he thrust towards the arc, I stopped my sword just under his blade. It had formed an X, and I slid my sword round horizontally, blade towards his sword hand and the hilt. Katanas have a small hole in the hilt where a *shodakashi* (small dagger) can be placed (neither of our swords had the dagger in). My left hand held my right as I thrust, and the blade's point reached its target; when I felt the point reach the dagger hole, I stopped thrusting.

Tony's red eyes showed shock and anger as he realised what I had done. The blue around me intensified as I glared back, and with a quick wrist action with my right hand, I flicked the sword from his grasp. As it started to move upwards, I grabbed the hilt with my left hand and spun it round. I held both blades and chopped towards him, forming an X round his neck. He gasped, and his eyes showed fear as my eyes flashed neon blue. I went in for the kill. My whole body had been tense, as I had gone into the kill mode some seconds earlier; it had been automatic. The two blades touched the bulging arteries in his neck and had just started to bleed when I realised what I was doing. Instead of pulling them together and across to take his head off in one swift movement, I stopped. I drew them back away from his neck and flipped my wrists so they stood straight in the air. My muscles bulged, and my body shook as I blazed blue, my temper flowing out.

Tony stepped back, red eyes dimming, his trembling fingers touching his neck to feel the cuts. Out of the kill mode now, I started to relax; the blue light dimmed, and I gently relaxed my body as I let the swords drop slowly to my sides. I shook my head.

Still in a trance, I heard Tony shouting, "Kevin, Kevin."

My eyes turned towards him, blazing as they met his. He stared at me, dumbfounded.

"Kevin, Kevin, where on earth did you learn to do that?" he asked.

Nearly back to normal now, I replied, "Just a little trick I learned up in Geordie land [Newcastle upon Tyne]."

"Your skill is truly remarkable," he said.

As I thanked him, I thought, *Maybe you'll think twice about fucking with me and show me a bit of respect.*

He extended his hand to mine to shake it and said, "I am overawed. Thank you; thank you for your demonstration and my chance to have a practice. I am honoured."

"*Arigat'o gozaimasu*" ("Thank you, sir"), I said as I bowed to him.

He pressed a bell on the wall, and within minutes, Justine (Shelta's cousin) arrived.

"My daughter, Justine, I believe you have already met," Tony said.

"Hi, Kev, nice to see you again," she replied.

"You too, Justine," I said, thinking how much she looked like Lisa Stansfield, the singer.

"Coffee and biscuits for two, my love, if that is alright by Kevin," Tony said.

"That's fine by me, Tony," I replied, thinking I must have gained some respect by him calling me "Kevin."

After Justine went for the coffee, he said, "Right, let's talk business. Kevin, please sit here."

I sat in the beautiful leather chair next to a small table that he pointed to; he sat in another chair opposite me.

As I opened my briefcase, I said, "I take it Mr Dent told you all about *Workforce*?"

"No need," he answered. "I know all about it, Kevin. I checked up on it last week; can't be too careful, you know. Anyway, as you have seen, what I do is a specialist trade, so I'd like to diversify my advertising to a larger audience, as it were, and your publication is perfect."

The door opened, and as Justine placed the coffee tray on the table, my first thought was, he was the last one I'd expect to do business with; funny old world, isn't it? I put milk and sugar in my coffee and said, "I'll show you the ads and the prices, if I may," as I got out my folder.

After I went through everything, he stated, "Well, Kevin, as I said, we are a very prestigious business, so we'll go for the inside front cover, in colour."

Oh joy and happiness. This was the most expensive ad we had, as the inside front cover was the first ad the punters saw. It cost two thousand pounds for a full page and counted as ten sales, as it was the most difficult to sell. I had just reached my whole sales target for the week. JR would have an orgasm. I had just made six hundred pounds, 10 × £50 per sale plus a hundred pound bonus; I had made seven hundred pounds for the week, with Graham's sale.

I was still smiling when he continued, "I also believe you do twelve separate issues nationwide, so if we can talk a discount, I'd like to be in all twelve."

Hardly being able to contain myself, I worked it out. 12 × £2,000 = £24,000 with a 17.5% discount (we would pay the VAT) = £19,800.

I quickly worked out I myself had just made £7,200 plus Graham's £100 = £7,300 for a week's wages; it was nearly four months' wages. Never mind JR having an orgasm; I was having one.

I told him the price; he smiled but never flinched at the amount and said, "I don't believe in banks, so will cash do?"

Fucking hell, JR will have a multiple orgasm over this, it was the biggest sale the company had made and cash as well. I couldn't wait to tell him. I signed all the documents, got the artwork, and gave Tony his copies. I stood up and said, "Thank you very much, Mr De la Wyle; it has been an absolute pleasure to do business with you" (and I meant it).

"It's been an education for me today, Mr D'Arcy; you must show me how to do some of them sword manoeuvres some time."

"Anytime you like, Tony," I replied sincerely. I shook his hand and said goodbye and headed towards the door.

"Just one thing before you go, Kevin."

Shit, I thought, *he's done all this for spite,* but he handed me the katana I had just been using with the shodakashi in it and continued by saying, "Please accept this gift as a token of my appreciation of your dazzling display."

As you will gather by now, I am never lost for words, but my mouth just went blah, blah, blah.

His grin went from ear to ear as he said, "I made it myself twenty years ago, so it's not as old as you think, but it's still as effective. I studied the exact way the samurai warriors made them, so it's a precise replica from the Ming Dynasty."

"Thank you again, Mr De la Wyle. I'll treasure it forever. It's so perfectly balanced; it could have been tailor-made for me. I'll be eternally grateful."

"You may be right on both counts, Mr D'Arcy," he said, strangely.

As I went to go to the car, I saw Justine down the passage, and she waved and smiled at me as I left. *This gets curiouser and curiouser*; I thought as I went over to TBWSB and opened the door. I sat down and switched her on; my heart was thumping. Nearly twenty thousand pounds in cash; JR Seven Bellies would have a multiple multiple orgasm. His wife Pat would never get his trousers clean, and I had personally made a small fortune. I couldn't wait to ring him.

Fuck him, I thought and put on "Born to be Wild" by Steppenwolf; it epitomised the way I felt. I looked at my watch: 12.26 and 3 seconds. I was never going to make my one o'clock; anyway, I had nearly twenty thousand pounds on me. Too risky to carry around. I'd go back to the hotel, put it in the safe, and ring the office. Miss Leeming went through my mind as Steppenwolf sang, "Born to be wild, born to be wild, born to be wi-wi-wild."

I looked at the beautiful Katana on the back seat. I decided to wait till I got back home and went on the beach in the early hours in the morning; me and Ziggy (my gorgeous little Jack Russell puppy) would have some fun, as she loves to watch me practise the martial arts.

I rang Miss Leeming from the car. "Miss Leeming, Kevin D'Arcy from *Workforce*. I'm ringing about our one o'clock appointment. I'm afraid I have to go back to Carlisle then Whitley Bay, so I'll have to reschedule you."

"Whitley Bay? Did you say Whitley Bay?" a posh, highly agitated voice asked.

"Yes," I said, "it's near Newcastle upon Tyne."

"Do you know Earsdon? It's near there."

"Of course I do; it's only a couple of miles away from me, Miss Leeming."

"Fuck the Miss Leeming; call me Fiona, and I'll call you Kev, if that's all right. It's just that's where I come from originally. Where are you staying? I need to talk to you now," she rattled on like an M15 machine gun.

"I'm staying at the George in Amesbury," I replied, "and I'll be there in five minutes."

"Right, see you there in half an hour," she said, hanging up without giving me a chance to answer.

The car park for the hotel appeared as I wondered what she wanted and as I turned into it I thought, well you will find out in half an hour. The car park was empty as I pulled up and stopped. I grabbed my briefcase, as I dare not leave it in the car with all that money in it; better safe than sorry. I locked the car, set the alarms, and headed for the reception; a Jack Daniels was in order to celebrate one of the best days of my selling career. Both Shelta and her mother were busy in reception.

"Morning, girls."

"Morning, Kevin," they both answered, giggling.

"You're back early," Iuatha said. "Any problems?"

"Quite the contrary. I've had a brilliant day up to now, but I was a bit behind time, so I arranged to meet a client here."

"I take it you'd like a drink then," Shelta said. "Jack Daniels, ice, slice of lemon, and a drop of lemonade; a double, I think, judging by your smile."

She's done it again, I thought as the butterflies danced round in my stomach. *Marry me and have my babies. God, I love you.* She walked through to the bar with me and gave me a curious sideward glance, her green eyes gleaming. *Yes* echoed in my head; I looked quizzically at her.

"Did you say yes?"

"Yes. Yes, I did say yes, Kevin."

She handed me my drink, I swallowed it in one and asked her, "Did that really happen, Shelta? Am I going mad?"

"Yes, it did happen, Kev; the matrix was formed last night, and our psychic bond will grow stronger and stronger. We are as one now; our souls are entwined."

I got whacked; it was the strongest whack I've ever had, like a crowd of people walking on your grave.

Inside, I shuddered from head to toe, as if I had just been touched by the cosmic gods. I started to say, "Shelta, my angel, we really must talk about this …," when I heard a voice I recognised shout, "Kevin D'Arcy, I presume. Fiona Leeming. Get the drinks in; mine is large vodka with coke and ice."

I instinctively looked at my watch: 13.00 and 0 seconds exactly, I then looked at her, and it struck me I had seen her before, back home.

"Same again for me, one of what the lady wants, and get one for yourself and your Mam, please, Shelta."

Fiona shook my hand and said, "Hunting Lodge, West Monkseaton. Dead right, I thought. I saw you there last year in the bar with a really cute little Jack Russell, doing funny tricks.

"Spot on, Fiona. I thought I recognised you, but I meet so many people in my game, it's hard to remember where." You could hardly miss her, though; once seen, never forgotten. She was short and cuboid, a mass of thick ginger hair, large blue eyes, and underneath her black and gold kaftan bulged the biggest pair of tits I've seen in a while. They made Shelta's tits look like nipples, and they looked big enough to feed ten babies for a week. I took to her immediately; she seemed to be a character, but mainly she was nice about my dog Ziggy, my hairy little angel, I called her.

As Shelta handed us the drinks I said, "Would you like to sit down, Fiona?"

"Cheers, just over there," she said as she grabbed my arm and steered me over to a corner table.

"Thanks, Shelta; see you later."

"Just shout if you want anything else, Kev," she replied as she walked into the reception.

"What a coincidence meeting here like this and both being from the same area, Kevin," remarked Fiona.

"Small world, isn't it?" I replied.

"Well, let's see what you've got to offer, and no bullshit. Mind, I am a businesswoman, you know, and then I want to ask a favour."

I got out my folder and started my spiel. Once I finished, she replied right off.

"I'll take the back cover in colour; it's a good position because people throw down magazines in an office or whatever, and they land backside up like a front cover, good for my business."

To quote Richard Meldrew, I did not believe this. Fifteen hundred pounds for an ad; it was worth seven sales, £350 bonus. My mind quickly computed the totals: £19,800 + £600 + £1,500 = £21,900, and my commission all together: £7,650.

"I'll pay by cheque, if that's okay," Fiona as she pulled out her chequebook. "I never carry cash."

Ah, well, can't win them all, I thought. Seven Bellies' underpants are never going to be clean once I tell him this. I'm going to have to tell him I must come back to Carlisle with all this money. He wouldn't object, as he would want his greedy fat paws on it. It also gave me a chance to get back to Sanity (Whitley Bay).

"That's fine, Fiona," I said, asking her to make the cheque out to *Workforce* as I handed her the contract. "Want another drink?"

"Large vodka and coke with ice, and a half of Guinness with flat coke in please, Kevin, that's in a pint glass, of course," she said.

"I'll go and have Shelta get the drinks; do you want a sandwich or anything? I do; I'm starving."

"Whatever sandwiches you are having will do me fine, Kev," she replied.

The Jack Daniels had gone straight to my head; my psychic senses seemed more attuned when I'd had a few drinks, so I tried a little test.

Shelta-Thari De'Danann, you unbelievably gorgeous shaggable creature, come here, please, I thought.

As if by magic, she appeared at the door. *Same again, you walking hormone?* She thought as she went round the bar.

It works, I thought and replied aloud, "Nearly, but I'd like half a Guinness in a pint glass and half a pint of flat coke to go in it."

"Yuck! That's not for you, is it? It sounds awful."

"No, it's for Miss Leeming over there." I grimaced and added, "Look, I'll order her a taxi after this, and then we must talk, please; it's important."

She put the tray with the drinks on it beside me and answered, "Okay, then, give me an hour."

I walked back to the table, gave Fiona her drinks, and asked what I could do for her, reminding her of the favour she had asked for.

"I take it you go back home on Friday, like all reps, so I was wondering if I could scrounge a ride with you there and back. I don't often get back home, so I thought this might be an ideal opportunity. If, that is, you don't mind."

I was thinking of going back home with all the money, and I was going to ask Shelta to come with me and meet the family and see where I lived. It's about an eight-hour drive, so we'd have had a long private talk. But what the hell? She had just made me £350, so how could I refuse?

"For you, dear, anything," I replied with genuine affection.

"That's cushty [Geordie for "good"]," she said, but in her posh voice, and carried on by saying, "Well, I must get back to work. Time is money, you know. Would you order me a taxi?"

"I'm going back tomorrow actually, if that's okay by you, so I'll pick you up about 7 a.m."

"Fine; see you then."

The telephone box was on the bar, and as I looked for a taxi number, Tony de la Wyle walked in.

"Good afternoon, Kevin, Miss Leeming; doing business, are we?" he asked.

"Yes, Tony, we've just finished, and I was looking for a telephone number for a taxi for Fiona."

"No problem, Kevin; my chauffeur is outside, and he's on his way to Salisbury, so he can drop Miss Leeming off."

"Marvellous, marvellous," cried Fiona.

Seeing Tony reminded me I had left the katana in the car, so I offered to walk her to the car park. She grabbed my arm and bustled me towards the exit, Tony following behind. As we entered the car park, there stood the big black Rolls-Royce I had seen on my first night, parked in stark contrast next to TBWSB. As I went over to the car, Tony ordered the chauffeur to take Fiona home and then walked over to me. The sword was in my left hand as I locked the car door with the remote control, putting the alarms on.

"Very impressive, Kev," he said as TBWSB went through the alarm sequence.

"So is your car, Tony, a real classic. May I buy you a drink? It's the least I can do in return for this amazing sword."

"I only drink one thing, Kev; it's very special and expensive. I have the only bottles but keep a few in reserve in the hotel cellar."

"Money is no object, Mr de la Wyle; in view of what you've paid today, I will pay whatever it is."

Shelta and Iuatha watched us walk in together, and I noticed a worried frown on their faces, especially Shelta's, as she saw the gleaming black and gold sword in my hand.

Don't worry, darlin', I telepathised to her and watched her face relax a bit. Tony took out a bunch of keys and went towards the cellar door.

"I'll be back in a minute; go in the bar and make yourself comfortable," he told me, disappearing down the stairs. As I walked towards the bar, Shelta beckoned me with her beautifully manicured finger.

"I'm going up to pack now; it's all arranged with my mother. I'd like an early night, so I'll meet you at your room at 6.30 a.m., and Kevin, please be careful."

"Don't worry, sweetheart," I said, completely ignoring the fact she had read my mind about going back home with me; it was becoming a common occurrence now. "This is Asmodeus, As, for short," I said, holding up the sword to show her (Asmodeus, the Persian devil of devilment, was the nickname I had just given it; the name seemed quite apt).

"What's borrowed must be returned, as you will learn, Kevin. Think of the matrix; my uncle doesn't give anything for nothing."

"With you and the matrix watching over me, Little Mother [now why did I say that? It just popped into my mind.], I have no need to worry."

"There is so much I have to explain to you, Kevin; be on your guard at all times. We'll talk tomorrow at your house after we drop Fiona off. Please don't mention any of this in front of her; it's too dangerous. Look, I must go, as I have lots to sort out before I leave."

Then she kissed me fully on the mouth. I could feel pure absolute love flowing through my whole being and into my soul.

"We are destined to be together, Kevin. The matrix has chosen us, and we have a role to play. I love you with all my heart and soul. I knew you were the one when I first set eyes on you. Iuatha told me my knight in shining armour would come on a great white charger to rescue me, so when I saw TBWSB pull up, yes, it was my mother in my uncle's Rolls-Royce that night in the car park, she told me you were here and you had felt her presence, so she knew you were psychic. Then when I saw you and you saw me, I knew we both felt love at first sight. Taliesin, the lord of the matrix (he became the lord in the highest sphere when Lucifer fell from heaven to hell), told me when you looked at me, 'Little Mother, he is here.' So you see what is happening, Kevin, Taliesin has blessed you also. It is destiny."

She gave me a quick peck on the lips and went upstairs. My mind was still reeling with what she had just told me when Tony interrupted my thoughts.

"Here we are, nectar of the gods: St. Secaire's mead, Druid's brew, we nicknamed it here. You had better enjoy it; it costs two hundred pounds a bottle."

Since I had just made seventy-two hundred pounds off him, it was petty cash, so I said, "No problem, Tony; have two if you want."

"That's very kind of you. I will; that's just the way the Druid Tetrachs [bosses] used to drink it: one bottle each. I will open this one for you and then go and get another one."

Some expensive piss-up ("drinking session" in Geordie) this is going to be; I could get drunk for a month up north on four hundred quid.

"Whatever you want, it is yours, Mr De la Wyle," I said politely.

"Be careful what you say, Kevin; that's the third rash statement you've made today."

Wanting to know why he was taking everything so literally, I asked, "And what three are they, Tony?"

His deep-set black eyes bore into mine (I got whacked again), and he very carefully said, "First, you said the sword could have been tailor-made for you. Second, you would be eternally grateful to me, and thirdly, whatever I want is mine. The sacerdotal powers of the Druids may grant me all three, if you're not careful."

He laughed at my reaction, but it was a menacing, cruel laugh, as I put my jaw back to where it had dropped from. As we sat down, he removed the plug from the stone jar and poured the mead into a superb gold goblet, embedded with blue stones; it looked very ancient.

"Beautiful, aren't they?" he asked, looking at the goblets. "They are original altar goblets from Stonehenge itself from the sacrificial altar; they date back to 300 BC. They are named the *Dovaidona Magi Droata,* which means 'the Blue Stone Goblets of Dovaidona.' The blue stones signify the fifty-nine blue stones at Stonehenge and are the equivalent number of days in two lunar months. The gold signifies the sun; Dovaidona was the oldest son of the Druid Master, who came here from France in 300 BC. Stonehenge had been in disuse for a thousand years when he and his family, the Tetrachs (twelve masters and priests and three hundred minor officials and villagers), took up residence. So why the son of the Druid Master, I can see you dying to ask. Well, he went onto higher things. The gods were pleased with his work, and he transmogrified into a higher being called Zomolxis, who could metempsychosis himself into an animal God. His name? Why, Toutaitis [it seemed to jump into my soul], and yes, I am a direct descendent of the original Toutaitis. De la Wyle was the name of the bishop who owned the abbey where I live now; we have been there for nine hundred years, generation after generation. Anyway, I will leave you with your thoughts while I go and get the other bottle."

Shocked and stunned by his speech, I walked over to the bar and helped myself to a neat Jack Daniels. I needed a double, after that tirade. I felt his speech was a warning of some kind, and my inner psyche instantly switched into the matrix (this is what I felt with Shelta last night), the transistor and battery theory. Me the battery, the matrix the transistor, both together to make the power, the music. I felt a slight jolt as we joined, and a warm glow spread through me (wait, was it Taliesin or the Little Mother or both? I had yet to learn).

Lost in the aura of the matrix, I came to as Tony banged the bottle of mead on the table and said, "Penny for them."

"Oh, you're back. Sorry, I was thinking about getting back home," I said, which wasn't a lie.

He poured mead into his goblet from his bottle, and then I poured mead into my goblet from my bottle.

"A Druid toast, I think," Tony said, an evil grin on his lips. "The rapid oak tree, before him heaven and earth quake. In every land his name is mine." He then drank his goblet of mead straight down in one.

I followed his leave and did the same. I was surprised; it was wonderful, a cross between warm rum and Southern Comfort. A warm glow spread right through me.

Then, bang, my insides, outsides, and every side seemed to explode like two volatile substances mixing together. Whatever this stuff was obviously didn't mix with the matrix tuned into my brain.

Utter surprise registered on Tony's face as I tensed all over; I don't think it had the desired effect he had hoped for.

I shook my head, said, "Ah, nectar. I'll have some more of that," and picked up the bottle. At two hundred pounds a bottle, I wasn't going to waste it, anyway, Geordies had a reputation for drinking, so I couldn't let the lads down. I poured some more in the goblet, and as I went to drink it, the stones took on translucence to them; the matrix, I thought: It was protecting me from the mead. Tony watched in awe as I swallowed the whole lot again. Whatever the matrix was doing, it was working. I didn't shudder this time, so I said, "Not joining me, Tony? It's paid for, you know."

His eyes were riveted to the stones on my goblet; scowling, he filled his cup and drank.

"Your toast this time, Kevin; that's the old way of doing it."

"May the bird of paradise fly up your nose, but never shit in your mouth." We both laughed; he's relaxing again, I thought.

We did four more toasts, and then Iuatha came in with the sandwiches I had ordered earlier. I thanked her and started eating them, as I was ravenous.

"Help yourself, Tony."

"Not for me," he said. "I've already eaten."

Iuatha came back and said, "Mr D'Arcy, phone call for you; a Mr Kent."

Shit, I'd forgotten all about *Workforce* in the excitement. "Excuse me, be back in a minute or so," I said to Tony.

I won't go into graphic details, but when I told Wurzel what had happened, even he was dumbfounded. He was on a bonus too, and he'd make about £750, so he was ecstatic. I explained it was nearly all in cash and that I would have to come back with it the next day; he agreed with me, for once. He also told me JR wasn't back yet. I got a mental picture of him telling Seven Bellies, the multiple orgasms beginning and spunk shooting all over the ceiling as he danced around the room, whooping with joy. As I put the phone down, I thought, *that'll give him something to think about.* I knew I'd be in the good books for a long time to come. When I walked back into the bar, I was smiling.

"Everything okay?" Tony asked.

"Handsome," I said (in a cockney accent, it means "good") and sat back down next to my sword, which I had left lying there on a bench (I almost forgot about it). "Where were we before I was so rudely interrupted?"

"Just about to have another drink," replied Tony. We filled our goblets and Tony started making a toast. "Thou born at Bayeux with Druids for ancestors," but my attention was drawn away from him by a buzzing noise, one to my left and one to my right. I quickly looked side to side and saw two rather large bluebottle flies. The one on my left started buzzing round me, while the one on the right, the larger one, hovered about ten feet away. I hate the dirty creatures, so I started to swat my hand at the one on my left. I had to put my drink down, as I was flicking so hard that I was spilling it. I suddenly got whacked again, and a voice (neither male nor female) seemed to echo in my mind:

Beware of the Ratapa.

Tony flinched and said, "I must go to the bar and get a drink of water; my mouth is dry with all the mead."

He stood up and moved towards the bar, and as he did, the larger fly on the right came flying towards me. Some hidden instinct in the recess of my mind made me move. My left hand grabbed the sheath of Asmodeus, and my right hand grabbed the hilt of the sword. In one very fast, fluid movement, it was out of the sheath and curving in an arc towards the bluebottle. It was instantly split in two, and a high-pitched shriek pierced the room as the blade went back into its sheath before its body hit the ground. Tony's head whipped round to face me just as Shelta came running in the door. Tony's eyes blazed with venomous fury.

"Kevin, are you okay?" Shelta asked.

"Fuck off, bitch," came this deep baritone voice from Tony's mouth, but it wasn't his voice; it sounded like the voice that came out of Regan's mouth in the film *The Exorcist.* His features shimmered, and his eyes started to glow red. It looked like he had two faces merging into one, his own and something like an animal. Zomolxis, the animal God.

"Let's go now, Kevin," Shelta said. "I'll drive if you let me, and we can ring Fiona up and tell her we'll pick her up on the way."

"Go? Go where, you fucking slut?" asked Tony's spectral voice, resonating around the room.

"I'm going away for a few days to Whitley Bay." As she stared at him, her huge green eyes started to emit an electric blue light. A blue aura shimmered round the contours of her body, and she said to Tony in a firm voice, "We are to be married, Uncle. The matrix has chosen us to undo the chaos and evil you created."

He went berserk; his body seemed to enlarge and grow more muscular and harder.

"You have betrayed the Derivest," his voice boomed, "thy sacred race from the temple of Belens; you whore of Taliesin from the matrix. You will suffer unspeakable pain and torture for this."

"Fuck me, what's going on round here?" I screamed at no one in particular; neither of them seemed to hear me.

The matrix started swirling round Shelta's head, and as the blue around her intensified in colour, she said, "Toutaitis De la Wyle, patriarch of the Tetrachs and evil guardian of the Ratapa, you have already taken one that I loved, Lugus De'Danann, my father, and I, Shelta-Thari De'Danann, will not allow you to take another. As you well know, my name means 'the secret dialect of the Sidhe race.' We, the De'Danann, the Sidhe race, will not allow you to create anymore evil."

So that's what her name means, I thought and watched in amazement as she plunged her fingers into the matrix. She arched her fingers down as she had done with me in the bedroom to tap me into the matrix, but this was surprisingly different. Electric blue lightning bolts were coming out of the swirling matrix forming on the end of her fingers, and as she arced them down, she pointed at Tony.

In an almost-mystical female voice, she said, "I use my name Shelta-Thari [secret dialect] to invoke the vengeance of the matrix of Taliesen against you, Toutaitis De la Wyle, possessor of the powers of Zomolxis. Now be gone, back to your own hell."

The lightning bolt hit him in a cacophony of sound and colour, like a thunderbolt hitting a tree. The air sizzled with electricity as his shape exploded in a mass of red, gold, and black colours. All that was left was a slight mist and an acrid, burning smell. I stood mesmerised, when Shelta grabbed me and brought me back to my senses.

"Quickly get your stuff packed. I'll ring Fiona and tell her to be ready. I'll make up some excuse about you having an emergency at home and that's the reason you have to go now. I'm already packed, and Iuatha will know what's going on. Now hurry."

I sobered up in a hurry, as I dashed up the stairs to pack.

Chapter 9

Back to Sanity (Whitley Bay)

I just grabbed everything, threw it in the suitcase, and stuffed what was left in some plastic bags. I had a quick look round to make sure I hadn't forgotten anything; the time flashed on the clock: 18.32 and 6 seconds. I looked out the window; it was dark. I saw a red glow in the distance; it was Stonehenge. It pulsated a blood red. I had a vision of Toutaitis standing at the altar, shaking with rage. His figure looked larger and broader. He had a red cowl wrapped round his head and was covered from the neck down with an electric blue robe. You couldn't see his face; there was just a black hole inside the cowl.

"Shelta soon fucked you off," I muttered to myself.

Then the vision of Toutaitis changed; two huge glaring red eyes appeared inside the cowl, and a voice boomed out in my head: *You will suffer, both of you. I curse you with the Broichan sacrifice to Artemis.*

I grabbed my stuff and ran for the door. "Just let me get back to Sanity," I prayed to anyone who was listening.

Shelta was waiting, holding my briefcase and Asmodeus the katana.

"Shit, I nearly forgot about those," I said as I grabbed the stuff from Shelta.

Seven Bellies would be livid it if I forgot the money; my life would be hell, as if it wasn't already. As we ran to the car, I flipped the remote control on, and TBWSB went through the motions of switching the alarms off. I opened the boot and shoved everything inside.

"Look, darlin', no disrespect, but TBWSB is very fast and temperamental; she takes some getting used to. I never let anyone drive her. I'm the only one who has, from buying her brand new."

"I understand, Kev; we need to get away quickly, and I know you're more than capable of doing that. I was just worried about the drink you've had, but wait." She touched me gently on top of my head with her right hand and closed her eyes. I felt the alcohol and my hangover disappear immediately.

"That's amazing. I feel great, wide awake and alert. How did you do that?"

"Paul Daniels [the magician] has nothing on me, but I only transferred it to myself to save time. I'll be a bit hungover for a while, but it might help me sleep. After the energy I've used, I'm drained and need to recharge my batteries."

"Well, if Fiona is tired and goes to sleep as well, I can concentrate on my driving. You also won't see how fast I am driving; it may make you nervous."

"Not with you driving," she said, giving me confidence.

I switched on the ignition, and TBWSB roared to life as if she knew there was trouble. I dimmed all the lights on the dashboard. I put on the CD of *The Private Music of Tangerine Dream* and selected track 2, "Too Hot for My Chinchilla," and track 6, "Rolling down Cahuenga," both excellent songs to drive to. I drove off and headed for the A303, then left to the A343 straight to Middle Wallop. There was a quicker way, but I wanted main roads so I could put my foot down. TBWSB went like greased lightning and looked like a white blur as she sped past everything. What a machine.

In the dim glow of the car, music blaring away, Shelta said, "Fiona will be waiting next to the post office on the Main Street; her cottage is right next door."

I saw her standing and waving, as she recognised the car. "What a to-do," she said as she got in the back seat.

I looked at the clock on the dashboard: 19.15. "We should be back in the early hours of the morning, depending on whether there's any traffic, speed traps, or coppers," I said.

Don't worry about speed traps or coppers, Shelta said telepathically, with a twinkle in her eyes. *It's been taken care of.*

I looked at her; she had used telepathy so Fiona wouldn't hear us.

You'll see, she added, smiling at me.

"Well, I don't know about you, but I'm shagged," Fiona muttered. "I'm taking a sleeping tablet."

"Okay, I'll wake you both up when we get there," I replied, noticing Shelta's eyes were closing. "Goodnight, ladies; sweet dreams," *and wet dreams to you, gorgeous,* I telepathised to Shelta; her smile turned mischievous.

With the synthesised tones of Tangerine Dream floating quietly out of the speakers, so as not to wake the girls, TBWSB blasted up the road. I thought about what Shelta had said earlier about speed traps and coppers. I was about to find out.

I had filled the tank with petrol at the garage next to Fiona's, so I knew we had enough fuel to get us home. I headed up the A343 going north, turned right on the A303 East, and then left onto the A34 Oxford Road going north. Left onto the M40 going north, right on A43 East and then left at Junction 15A onto the M1 going north back to Sanity. I looked at the tripmeter that I had set to zero at the start; we had covered just over a hundred miles, and the time was 20.21 and 28 seconds. We had averaged 80 mph. I instinctively looked at the fuel gauge; it hadn't moved, which was curious. I tapped it, but it stayed where it was. *Strange,* I thought. The M1 was quiet, it being a Tuesday night, and most of the rush hour traffic had gone. I guessed we had about two hundred miles to go, and with a clear road, I could put my foot down. It was motorway all the way. M1, M18, left onto the A1M back to Newcastle, and then just down the main road to Whitley Bay.

I patted the Super Bitch's dashboard and said to her, "Well, Baby, let's test out Shelta's theory."

The clock jumped up to 110 mph; she purred like a dream. All you could hear was the noise of the tyres against the highway. She was cruising up the road like a spaceship in flight, flying through the night, her white bodywork gleaming in the overhead lights. As I neared 125 mph, I knew there were traffic cameras up ahead.

"Ah, well, here we go, theory time," I mumbled.

There was a slight blue flash as we neared the camera, and I noticed the front bonnet of the car had a blue hue to it. That's what it must be; the matrix had enveloped us like in *Star Trek*, when they put the shields up to protect it. The blue flashes on the cameras continued all the way up to the A1M. *Damn clever, these Druids,* I thought as I turned left on the A1M North.

The time was 21.21; we had covered another hundred miles, doing over 100 mph. Well, the test really began then, as we had just over a hundred miles to go; there weren't many cameras on the A1M, but there were loads of police patrol cars. Funnily enough, a lot of people thought TBWSB was a police car, as she looked like one of the cars they used on the motorways, the Sierra Cosworth, but without the lights and logos.

I looked over at my beautiful Shelta, and she smiled in her sleep, those wonderful red lips of hers pouting, and I wondered if she'd read my thoughts again. The roads were quiet again as I put my foot down, 100, 110, 120 mph. "God, I love this car," I said, patting the dashboard affectionately as I looked at the fuel gauge again.

Still full, I thought. *Must be bloody good stuff, this matrix power.*

The Super Bitch seemed to glow brighter blue, as if agreeing with me. She seemed to be more silent than usual as we motored on towards Catterick. Now this was a bad section of road up to Scotch Corner, as you got loads of coppers around there. There on the right-hand side was a Sierra Cosworth, ready to pounce. I looked at the speedo: 127 mph. Their car was facing me, and they flashed their lights. I flashed back and saw one of them wave his hand at me in recognition. I flashed again to acknowledge them. Oh well, we passed the test; no blue lights flashing, so I carried on. What I didn't know was the vision the coppers had seen was TBWSB as a carbon copy of their own car, and inside their car, a voice said, "Police car in pursuit; have a nice night, lads. Over."

We went past Scotch Corner, and I saw sign saying Newcastle was sixty miles away; nearly back to Sanity. Forty minutes later, I was going down the A194 to the turnoff for the A19 to Jarrow and the Tyne tunnel (the tunnel which goes under the River Tyne, linking North and South Tyneside). We came out the other side (North Tyneside), and I paid the man in the tollbooth.

I turned right onto the A19 North and sped up the road. I felt invincible as the matrix protected us, and TBWSB seemed to like it. Shelta and Fiona awoke at the same time.

"Nearly home, girls. Earsdon's just along the road, Fiona, and my house is just one mile away from hers, Shelta, so we won't be long."

I turned right at the Holystone roundabout and headed down the A186 to Earsdon.

"Left at the roundabout, then first right, then left again at the next roundabout, and stop on the left," Fiona said, barking out directions.

"Yes, ma'am," I said in my best American accent.

"Just here, just here, turn next left," she ordered again.

I turned into the drive of a magnificent bungalow, all in its own grounds. I stopped outside a building all in glass at the side; it was an indoor spinning pool, complete with bar, showers, and changing rooms. It was a ranch-style bungalow, and it was huge; it must have cost at least £280,000 (prices are cheap in Geordie land).

"It's mine," said Fiona, "but the Wicked Witch, that is, my mother, also lives here. I'll tell you the story sometime; suffice to say, I inherited a bundle, but it's in trust bonds.

I handed her my personal business card with my home and mobile number on and said, "Give me a ring, and we'll have a drink over the next few days. If not, we're travelling back on Sunday."

"Okay, bye, and thanks a lot, you two. See you later," she said as she wobbled to the door.

I turned the car towards the dual carriageway to West Monkseaton. "Fancy a drink in the Hunting Lodge, beautiful," I asked Shelta. "We've still got time for last orders."

"Jack Daniels, ice, and lemonade would be like the nectar of the gods," she replied.

I turned right into the car park and stopped outside the bar. I looked at my watch: 22.15. It had only taken three hours, the trip odometer read 333 miles, and the fuel gauge was still full. I couldn't believe it; we had averaged 111 miles an hour, never got caught, and I still had a full tank of petrol.

Shelta smiled knowingly and said, "I told you it had all been taken care of."

"God, I love you, woman. Give us a kiss, you mucky ["rude" in Geordie] lass."

We kissed passionately, and I felt as though I was in heaven; no one would ever believe what had happened to me today. We got out of the car, and I set all the alarms. No one would touch her here, anyway; TBWSB was too well known, but there was over twenty thousand pounds in the boot. Better safe than sorry. As we stepped in the foyer, I could just imagine the faces of the men and women when they got a deck ("look" in Geordie) of Shelta-Thari De'Danann. I would have some fun with them trying to pronounce her name. I walked through the door first and saw my mate Mick Fryer sitting at the bar.

"Hey, Kev; you're back early, mate. No bother, is there?" he asked, sipping his pint.

Then, Shelta walked in. I wish I'd had a camera; this was classic. The whole pub went silent; they stopped drinking, and their jaws nearly hit the ground. I grabbed her hand and walked over to the bar where Mick sat. His eyes and everyone else's were out on stalks as they watched Shelta glide across the floor with feline grace. Mick eyed her up from head to toe. She had on a black micro skirt, which made her legs look as though they went on forever, and a white halter top that might as well have been a bra. Her breasts swayed side to side as they moved; the halter top accentuated them even more. Her green eyes widened and sparkled, and her long platinum hair swayed from side to side on her back. This lady could sure make an entrance; she knew she was beautiful but not in an arrogant way. It was me who felt arrogant, as I was with her and was as proud as punch. You could see all the blokes drooling over her, and their wives and girlfriends glaring at them for doing so.

"Want a drink, Mick?" I asked. "I'm buying. Same as usual for us, darling."

"Pint of Worthy [Worthington Bitter]," Mick replied, grabbing Shelta's hand and murmuring, "*Enchanted, mademoiselle. Je m'appelle Michael*" ("Enchanted to meet you, miss. My name is Michael").

"Another Geordie smoothie," Shelta said, laughing, as she gazed into Mick's blue eyes. "I'll have to watch myself."

Mick was tall and slim, with light grey hair and sparkling blue Paul Newman eyes. He was my best friend and a proper gent. Just then, Doreen the barmaid (the Snorting Dwarf) caught my eye.

"Two double Jack Daniels, ice, and lemonade, and a pint of Worthy, please."

Now this was a freak of nature, hence the reason for the nickname the Snorting Dwarf. It was hard to believe she and Shelta were the same sex. Everything Shelta was (tall, elegant, beautiful, pure femininity), Doreen was the opposite: short, scraggy, ugly, flat breasted, mousy brown hair, a mouthful of rotten teeth, and the nastiest attitude of anyone I've ever known. That explains the dwarf bit; the snorting was because she snorted whenever she laughed, hence the Snorting Dwarf.

She walked straight by me, as usual, and Mick (Mental Micky was his nickname, as he was such a laugh) said, "Same as usual."

Doreen and I can't stand each other, so she gets her own back by not serving me.

I noticed out the corner of my eye that there was a wicked smile spreading across Shelta's face. *I'll handle this little wart on the arse of humanity,* she telepathised over to me.

God help her, I thought.

Just then, George Gray, the manager, saw me from the other bar.

"Hiya, son; what'll it be? Nice to see you and your lovely lady friend."

He grinned when he got a glimpse of my little darling. I ordered what I had before and asked George to get one for himself. This was Gorgeous George, a proper gent: a smallish, stocky bloke (he was an ex pit man), a shock of short but beautifully curly black hair, in his early fifties, and lovely smiling brown eyes that always make you feel welcome in his presence. He was the epitome of a fine host.

As he handed up the drinks, he said, "Cheers, son; that'll be £7.10 with mine. I see the little bitch is up to her tricks again."

This time, Shelta did not smile. "No problem, George. I'm used to it by now." I watched Shelta's eyes get a small blue spark in them. *You're going to get it now, Snorter,* I thought.

Doreen walked past us again, nose up in the air and her rotten teeth gripped tight as she glared at Shelta. She was really jealous. In the film *Scanners*, when telepaths hone in on someone, for some unknown reason, they bleed. Well, here we go. Shelta's eyes glared at her with pure malevolence, and the Snorting Dwarf shuddered under her hypnotising glare. All of a sudden, her nose started to dribble blood, and then it gushed. Her beige miniskirt, showing her knobbly stick insect legs, suddenly seemed to go stripy red.

"Fucking bastard, fucking shit," she screamed, trying to block blood oozing from her nose and her legs. Then the front of her skirt seemed to explode with a red sunburst on the front (right next to her tadger).

Rick (Hook Nose) Homer, the local butcher, shouted, "Fuck me, what a stink," as a pungent aroma of rotten fish floated through the bar.

Doreen, totally embarrassed, ran out the back to try and clean herself up. *No chance of that,* I thought.

Hook Nose was his usual miserable self as he shouted across the bar, "Smells like the fish quay on a sunny afternoon because of that dirty little bitch."

Mick, Shelta, and I burst into fits of laughter, not at Hook Nose, who thought he was funny, but at what had happened to Doreen. Mick, by the way, was also psychic, and somehow, Shelta must have included him in this, a sign she liked him. I was glad. Just then, Derek Phillips walked in the bar door, as always looking as though he owned the place.

"Uh-oh, Fuck Face Phillips is in," I said to my two friends.

His eyes lit up as he saw us, or should I say Shelta. God made four cheeks in human beings, in Derek's case; he only made two and made him into a complete arsehole. He was a barristers son, bore an incredible likeness to John Hurt (who I really admire), and thought he was God's gift to women. I imagined what Shelta would do to him and then thought, *I wonder if Taliesin would allow me to do something to the obnoxious creep.*

As is by magic, "The Teacher" by Jethro Tull came on the jukebox, and Shelta said in my mind, *Yes, he will, and I have a way of doing a Doreen on him.*

Derek was a bigger version of John Hurt, but he had gone to seed, too much booze. He had that sallow complexion drinkers have and really bad breath. The clothes he wore put a tramp to shame, as all his money went to booze. He thought of nothing else apart from his cigarettes, but he still thought he was the bee's knees.

Why Fuck Face, then? You ask yourself. Well, he thought he had a dead sexy face; we all thought it was fucked up, hence the nickname.

"Hi, Kev. Hi, Mick." (Eyes lusting.) *"Hi-i-i, gorgeous,"* he oozed all over her, his hand going straight over her bum to pat it.

Here we go, I thought. Shelta bent forward slightly, and her skirt, which was just covering her bottom half, rose slightly, and her golden curls and her love lips peeked out. We were standing side by side by her now, Mick and I, so no one else could see her sexy bits. As Derek's fingers slid down the crease of her bum, they met with her wet hairy lips jutting out. Fuck Face's face was a picture, as his eyes nearly popped out his head, and his jaw dropped. Shelta wiggled her bum and her fanny like a little rabbit's tail, while Derek's fingers just caressed her inner lips. Derek stood mesmerised as she stroked the front of his trousers, and his prick rose. Fuck Face's claim to fame was he was hung like a donkey; he was. It was like a baby's arm. The pinpoint of blue appeared in her eyes as she looked at me and smirked.

Fuck Face stepped back as the front of his trousers started to expand rapidly, the zip on his rangy trousers straining. The pressure was enormous as Derek's prick bulged out, and the zip gave in to the strain. It lunged out like a cobra striking and stood up, all twelve and a half inches of it, straight and proud. The whole pub was looking at Derek now standing, dumbfounded, locking at his throbbing member.

He looked at Shelta, and she smiled. Mick and I were laughing our heads off as Fuck Face's right hand went down, and he grabbed hold of his shaft and started masturbating furiously. Everyone just gaped at Derek as his hand went up and down like a piston. Shelta winked at Mick and I as we stood next to her, facing Derek. She stared him straight in the face as his eyes rolled and his tongue hung by the side of his mouth like a dumb puppy. He couldn't stop as she licked her lips lustfully and ran her hand over her belly and under her skirt, lifting it slightly, showing her mound of gold and the pink fleshy lips of her love hole.

Shit, I think Fuck Face is going to get some scampi, I mused as Shelta eased her middle finger into her cleft. Derek went faster at the sight of this, but no one else could see what Shelta was doing, as we covered her sides, and Derek covered her front.

His knees started to tremble in the throes of an orgasm as she took out her wet finger, put it in her mouth, and sucked it in and out like a prick. That was it; Fuck Face flinched at the sight of this. God was she horny, as I well knew; even I was getting horny just watching her. Later, perhaps, I thought.

"Thar she blows," I shouted. I couldn't help it, as I knew he was ready to blow his lot. It started with a little spurt as it came out, and then it exploded in a white creamy stream.

"Well, the pub needs doing up a bit, but I hope Gorgeous George is going to pay Derek for artexing the ceiling," I said to my two friends. All the people were transfixed in amazement; women were muttering, "What a perv," and lots of other things like that, as Fuck Face gasped and groaned in orgasmic delight.

Not finished yet, Shelta grabbed him from the side and twirled him round as the last drops were dripping to the floor. "Come dancing, Derek," she said, twirling him round for everyone to see. "Whoops, I think you already have."

Fuck Face went round in a spin and fell to the floor, dizzy with what was happening and the amount of drink he already had. He fell to the floor in a heap, his donkey knob hanging down his leg like a limp rag, covered in white spunk dribbling down his leg.

Gorgeous George came running in as Derek flopped back, exhausted. "You dirty perverted creep," he snapped. "I always knew you were a wanker, but now you've gone and proved it. You're barred for life." He turned to me and Mick, and asked us to take him outside, away from the punters.

As Mick and I supped up and walked towards Fuck Face and Gorgeous George, I told Shelta, "Come on, darlin'. I think we've had enough fun for one night. Let's make tracks. My house is just round the corner."

She glided across the floor like a catwalk model, oozing her sexuality as she departed through the door.

I bet there will be a few more wanking tonight, I thought, *not over their wives*, as Mick, George, and I dumped Fuck Face Phillips in the car park, where he belonged. We left him in a heap, out of sight behind the beer kegs.

"Night, Kev. Night, Shelta," Mick said as he walked over to his house; he lived next to the pub. "See you tomorrow."

"Best laugh I've had in ages, Mick; give you a ring about eleven o'clock in the morning," I replied, opening the car door for Shelta. As the car alarms subsided, I said, "Boy, you are some lady; what do you have in mind next?"

Giggling, she said, "Just wait and see," and pointed to her nose, tapping it.

We were home in two minutes, and as I parked TBSWB in the drive of my cul-de-sac, I heard Ziggy, my pup, barking furiously. "My Mam must have dropped her off earlier," I remarked to Shelta. "She's the best little alarm in the world; she knows the sound of TBWSB."

As I opened the door, there she sat, crouched in the kitchen doorway. I love this pup so much, it hurts. My little hairy angel, as I call her, sat there, bum up in the air, front paws down, with her head resting on them, eyes watching the door, growling. I entered first; she tensed, ready to spring at whoever was coming in; she wasn't scared of anything, like most Jack Russell's. They have to be the best dogs in the world. She saw it was me and went wild, as usual. This beautiful little creature was so cute and funny, she was unreal. She flew at me as I bent down to kiss her; she licked my face and then ran off back into the kitchen. This was her mad half now, as I called it. She ran round like a whirlwind. Out of the kitchen, into the dining room, and back at me, barking, as I said, "I'll get you, mind." She then flew out, barked again, and then ran up to the top of the stairs and stood on the landing, yapping with excitement. What a little character she was. Then Shelta entered.

Ziggy stood transfixed as she watched me cuddle Shelta to my side. Now, this little pup either liked you or hated you; no in between. If she liked you, you could stay; if she didn't, you got out of the house quick because she'd bite your ankles or, even worse, your bum. Fuck Face Phillips still had the scar on his bum from where she bit him; good judge of character, that dog. I knew Shelta was a hit with her as she stood and did one of her favourite tricks. She sat back on her bum and reached her paws out in front of her, crossed together. She then lifted them up and down like shaking hands; this is what we called "Please, please, please." I could feel Shelta's heart melting as mine always did when I saw Zig do this.

I heard Shelta's voice in my mind, projecting into Ziggy's mind:

Come on, darling; I won't hurt you. My name's Shelta and I'm here to love and protect you and Kevin. Come on, give me some love.

I smiled as I watched Zig drop her paws back on the floor and cock her head to one side, ears up like a little fox, her beautiful brown eyes looking puzzled. Shelta crouched down to receive her, and Zig bounded down the stairs and jumped into her arms, snuggling into her ample breasts and licking her face furiously. All I could see was a mass of platinum hair cascading down; every now and again, a part of Zig was visible through it. Finally exhausted, Zig jumped down and stood in between us, barking with joy. There was hardly any make-up left on Shelta's face. The pup had licked her so much, only a tiny trace was left.

"Come on, up them stairs, or I'll bite your bum," I said as Zig went up them three at a time, barking excitedly.

"Will you bite my bum if I'm a bad girl?" Shelta asked in a little girly voice.

"I'll bite your bum," I replied, "eat your pussy, lick you out, suck you off, anything you want, anytime, anyplace, anywhere, just call me your Martini Fuck."

I ushered her up the stairs to the bedroom. As she walked up ahead of me, I could see right up her skirt, her perfectly rounded bum swaying from side to side and just a glimpse of her pubic hair with her swelling piss flaps peeping out.

My groin ached as I looked, and she turned her head round and smiled as she bent forward a bit and shook her bum, making her pussy look like a rabbit's tail again. The one-eyed milkman (my prick) was about to make a delivery, the fastest milkman in the north-east. Zig was jumping, yapping, and twirling up and down on the bed as we entered my bedroom. I dumped the cases in the small bedroom next door, switched on the hi-fi, and poured both of us a large vodka and lemonade with a slice of lemon. I thought I'd drop a hint to Shelta, so I selected "Feel like Making Love" and put it in the hi-fi's CD player.

"Wow," Shelta said, "that's some system." She watched in amazement as my Aiwa ZD3100M lit up. The sound out of this baby was phenomenal. It looked like the flight deck of Concorde as the four speakers blasted out Paul Rodgers' perfect voice and the spectrum analyser danced away on the screen with every note.

What a voice, and what a sound; she squealed with delight as I cuddled and stroked my little hairy angel (Ziggy). Shelta began stripping to the music and then giggled and said in her little girly voice, "Okay, Kev, I take the hint; come on and fuck me."

She then grabbed her tits with one hand and stroked her wide-open pussy with the other. My prick nearly jumped out and spat in her eye, and as I positioned her gently on the bed, a vision of Fuck Face Phillips came to mind, him wanking like a mad thing, and I fell over on my side, tears of laughter running down my face.

The pup started jumping all over me, thinking something was wrong.

"It's all right, darlin'," I said as I got up and took her next door to lie her on her bed. "Go to sleep, my little hairy angel. I'll see you in the morning."

She rolled on her back and did her "Please, please, please" trick, her beautiful eyes sparkling as I stroked her belly. Happy and contented, I covered her with her blanket and said, "Be a good girl, now; we'll see you in the morning."

Shelta appeared beside me, walked over to Ziggy, and kissed her on the forehead. Ziggy licked her as if to say thanks, and Shelta gently stroked the side of her face. The pup seemed to smile (she did that) and immediately went to sleep.

More magic? I thought.

"I haven't hurt her," she said, looking straight in my eyes. "I only thought with all the noise and the moaning and screaming, it might keep her awake, so I helped her go to sleep."

"All the moaning and screaming? What moaning and screaming?"

"You'll find out," she said as she grabbed my prick and led me into the bedroom.

She lay on the bed, legs wide apart, her hair spread across the pillows like a golden blanket. She smiled, licked her lips, and pouted lustfully as the next track, "Can't Get Enough of Your Love," came on the CD.

My stomach flipped, and my heart flooded with love for her. *A goddess; well, she very nearly was, wasn't she?* I thought as she lay there teasing me, massaging her left breast; her nipples were standing up like a dustbin on a hill, and her right hand stroked her wide-open, glistening hole. She blew me a kiss and spread opens her cunt lips; they sparkled like wet butterfly wings.

As I looked at her golden mound and the moist pink flesh inside, I said, "Scampi and tartare sauce for supper, I take it."

"Shut up and fuck me," she said.

"Don't you just love when they talk dirty," I replied as I sprang on top of her, kissing her passionately. "Just a minute," I said, sliding over to the hi-fi; I turned one of the knobs, put a tape in, and handed her a microphone.

"You're not sticking that up me, are you?" she asked, eyes widening in dread.

"Don't treat me like Fuck Face Phillips the perv," I replied, pressing the record button.

"Well, well, what are you going to do with it?" she asked, lips trembling.

"There's a karaoke system on the hi-fi," I explained, "so you can put your voice on top of the music and record it at the same time."

"You want me to sing to you when we make love? Oh, how sweet."

"Well, not quite," I said. "You're going to have a quadraphonic orgasm."

"What the fuck is that?"

"You'll see," I said, laughing menacingly as I slipped on top of her.

I dug my fingers in her hair, gently stroked her head and ears and neck, and then kissed her forehead, eyes, and mouth. I put my hands down and raised myself up on top of her, still kissing her, tongue my probing her mouth, hers doing the same, hungrily. As the music echoed round us, I positioned my prick on the entrance to her hole. I felt the top of my prick nudge the hairs, and it tickled it, making it throb more. I could feel my end touching the flaps, and as I eased forward, the lips were so wet, I slipped straight in.

I slid in slowly, easing myself up as I did so, so the shaft expanded her mound as it swallowed my prick. It felt so lovely and wet and warm as it slipped in; she squeezed her fanny muscles and her arse muscles so her inside love tunnel gripped it tighter round my prick, it felt wonderful. As I pumped up and down, you could hear our genitals squelching together in rhythmic delight; our hips pounded together in perfect unison. Shelta's head thrashed from side to side as she moaned and gasped and raked my back with her nails. The top of my prick kept tickling her clitoris, which stood up hard and erect as

I slid up and down on it. I knew we were both about to come; I could feel my spunk rising like oil in a borehole about to explode. Shelta's gasps grew quicker and quicker, and her hole got wetter and wetter, as the squelching increased with our ardent fervour.

"T-t-t-take the microphone," I gasped. "Let me hear you orgasm." As she moaned louder, her orgasmic cries echoed around the room on top of the music, through the four speakers. "Thank God the neighbours are away, and I've got double g-g-glazing," I stuttered, as both of us started to climax together.

We both came at the same time, my hot spunk bursting out inside her and her love juices squirting out of her lips, down her legs, bubbling and frothing with mine. We both groaned as the waves of pleasure flooded out with our juices, but Shelta's groan of orgasmic ecstasy echoed 400 watts of pure pleasure in a cacophony of sound round the room.

"I'm arriving, I'm arriving," she moaned into the microphone.

"I've come," I said, laughing with her; the sound vibrated all around the room. As we snuggled in together, ready to sleep after a long day, I looked at Shelta and said, "Well, back to Sanity; how do you like it so far?"

"There are some strange ones round here, Fuck Face, Hook Nose, and the Snorting Dwarf, but I like Gorgeous George and Mental Micky. But I really don't like ignorant bitches and pervs, so I'm going to put Fuck Face Phillips and Doreen the Snorting Dwarf in their place."

Uh-oh, I thought, hearing the menace in her chuckling voice. "And how do you propose to do that?"

"By mind mix," she replied, quite casually. "Just go to sleep, and when you wake up tomorrow, you'll know. Goodnight, handsome; sleep well, and let the matrix of Taliesin protect your soul." She kissed me passionately and then immediately went into a trance. I looked at her beautiful, angelic face; her hair spread out like golden tendrils beside her, and kissed her forehead.

"Goodnight, my little darlin," I answered and started to drift off. *Mind mix, what's a mind mix, never mind, I'll find out tomorrow* bounced round in my brain as sleep engulfed me.

Chapter 10

The Mind Mix

Morning, Shelta, I heard as I awoke with a start. It was still dark in the room as I had thick velvet curtains up to keep the sun out of the room. I looked at the digital clock, and on the hi-fi, it said 10.00 and 6 seconds. *I wonder where that woman's voice came from* went through my mind as I reached down to scratch my balls, as I had a terrible itch down there. I had kicked the covers off in the night so I could get straight to my itchy balls. I curved my fingers to have a good howk ("good go at it" in Geordie). My fingers just went squelch as they hit hair and a damp fleshy thing.

"Fuck me! Someone's cut me balls off," I screamed in a high-pitched voice.

My hands went up to my head to shake my brain awake. There was a tickling down my back and shoulders and chest; I took no notice, as my mind was screaming, *Where's me prick? Where's me balls? Someone's cut off my shagging tackle.* My hands came up to my chest and bounced off something quite large, round, and fleshy. I stopped and cupped my hands to my chest and felt a large curved tit with a lovely, tweak able nipple. "What the fuck?" I said as I shook my head to fully wake myself up. Tendrils flew all over, back and forward across my face and body. *A giant spider had got me, cut my balls off, and laid its eggs in me,* my mind screamed.

"I said, Good morning, Shelta," said a slightly deep, slightly posh Geordie voice that sounded very familiar.

''Who the fuck are you ''said a feminine voice which also sounded familiar. Then, I realised it was me who had said it. The curtains flew open, and I blinked my eyes to refocus them to the bright lights. As I rubbed my eyes to get the sleep out of them, I noticed a reflection

in the mirror on the dressing table doing the same thing. When my eyes fully focused, I was staring at Shelta-Thari. My right hand went up to my chest; the reflection followed. My hand grasped a right tit and shook it; the reflection did the same. Mind mix; she's done the mind mix. "You'll find out in the morning," she had said, and I had definitely found out. I was Shelta-Thari, and she was me. I looked at the female reflection in the mirror, and my mind was reeling; that's you. I saw her head turn, hair swirling over the left shoulder as I turned my head or her head or whatever. God, this was a lot to take in; my mind was so confused. I gazed at myself standing by the bed. My body of Kev was standing scratching its face; well, I did have a heavy growth.

"Oh, that's a bit rough, and I don't know how you can stand this thing hanging down, slapping against your leg," Shelta said, holding my prick in her hand, his hand, well, you know what I mean. She shook it round, aimed it like a hose pipe with the other hand, jiggled the balls up and down.

"Watch the old three-piece suit [cock and balls]," I said to myself from Shelta's body in her voice.

She looked at my body and stroked it all over, poking and prodding dead curiously.

"Hey, that's mine you're mucking about with," I said in a girlish voice. God, this was weird.

"Well, just watch what you're doing with my lovely soft bits and pieces; I'm not as hard and as muscular as you, so think before you act; that's part of the mind mix."

Whoa, I never thought of that. I'd have to remember for the moment, I was Shelta-Thari, not myself. If I got carried away, still thinking I was me, I could seriously damage her. I looked in the mirror and saw her body in a different light, not like last night me, looking lustfully at her, for now I *was* her. Well, if she could poke about my body, I would poke about hers. I had all her feelings and senses, but I was feeling them with my mind. The skin I had felt last night with my own hands felt completely different now, as I started to play with myself, well, herself.

"Hey you be careful with my shagging tackle," she said, mimicking me exactly; she was really into the part.

I fluttered my eyelids, cupped my breasts, and thrust them upwards; great, I could even suck my own nipples, and her tits were so well proportioned. I pouted at me (Kevin), mimicked her blowing a kiss, and twirled round. I jutted my bum up in the air as I bent over and wiggled my fanny like a little rabbit's tail, as I had seen her do with Fuck Face. I straddled my legs and bent straight down, hair touching the ground and my breasts hanging down, bouncing against my arms, swaying as I shuffled backwards and forwards.

My upside-down face smiled as I turned my upturned face round to smile at my alter ego. I flexed my right hand, extending my long slim middle finger, red talon glowing as I slipped it between my legs, sliding up to the top crease of my bum and easing down the split to meet the mutton button. I made her green eyes widen as I teased the piss flaps open wide and prised them open even further by using the other hand and finger. You could see my fanny, in all its glory, wide open, wet and willing; the feeling was superb. My whole body tingled from head to toe; every square inch was tingling with pure sexuality. This lady was a pure loving machine, made for sex, and I was honoured to be allowed to share this experience.

Come on, ladies and gents, how many of us have thought, *I wonder what it would be like to swap roles for a day*? A woman to a man and man to woman, just for one day, to see and feel what it's like. We've all wondered it, haven't we? Well, it was happening to me, and it brilliant. My finger eased into the split up to the clitoris. Fuck me, my knees startled to tremble as I felt my body quiver with sheer pleasure. Shelta looked at me, and her trouser snake started to rise; well, me, acting like a pure slut, and knowing my alter ego, how could the trouser snake refuse?

"Jesus is that what it feels like?" she asked, as it rose to touch her belly button. She reached down and stroked it, touching all the veins bulging out, ready to pump the spunk. "Can we …," she said, eyeing my wet split, squelching away as I felt my insides wet and warm. How could she resist? "You're a first-class slut, Kevin, you know that?" she said as she grabbed my hips and thrust straight into me.

Fucking hell, he's nearly splitting me in two, I thought as she rammed into me. *Hold on, Shelta; be gentle. I'll not piss for a week if you carry on like this.*

Sorry, Kev; it feels so weird fucking my body but feeling what you feel. My pussy is so tight and wet and warm, and your shaft is so hard and slippery. I can feel my insides as your shaft slips in and out.

Wait just a minute, I thought. *This is unreal.*

I could feel my shaft slipping in and out; her fanny was lovely and tight, and I could feel it all wet and warm as it slipped in and out of me. I groaned loudly as she moved her hand round and down my belly and had started flicking my hard little clitoris with her finger; it sent wonderful tingling feelings all through my body (for the time being, to stop confusion, I'll call it my body, Shelta's body, that is). Kevin used all his fingers to open the lips of my fanny from the front; my lips widened, and I could feel him stroking my clit and the fleshy hood. My bum and fanny tightened, and I could feel his wet, hard shaft pumping in and out, making squelching noises and the sound of slapping as his thighs whacked against the cheeks of my bum.

I can feel the spunk rising in my prick, she thought. *It feels tremendous, and the sensation of my prick going in and out of your fanny is great.*

"Well, if you're about to come, so am I," I gasped as waves of pleasure ripped through my body; the orgasm inside me was coming in like a tsunami.

Kevin's pace increased as he was about to come. I could feel his knob throbbing as he slapped harder and harder against my arse and fanny. I felt his balls tighten as they plopped against my fanny hole and love lips. Wrapped round his shaft, I could feel him coming as I tensed my arse muscles and my fanny gripped his prick tighter. We both came at the same time, and I could feel the warm sticky spunk spurting inside me as my juices flowed out; it felt divine.

Now, I know every man has a feminine side and vice versa, but this was weird. I liked it, a lot. I was getting worried I liked it too much. As Kevin pulled out his soaking wet prick, it went pop in my fanny; my piss flaps started slapping together like a seal, and it started making farting noises as the spunk and my love juice sprayed out. Kevin stood back, laughing, and his prick swung from side to side, dripping juices all over.

"So that's what they call the Farting Fanny," he said as I bent over to look at my cunt in the mirror, making farting noises as the juice ran down my legs. It felt so strange down there.

"That was absolutely incredible," I said as I shoved myself up against Kevin, rubbing his prick with my wet sticky mound, my breasts poking against his chest. The nipples stuck out like two walnuts as they prodded the hairs on his muscular chest; it sent shivers through my whole body, and my fanny throbbed. *This woman is just one big sex machine, a walking hormone,* I thought as her whole body ached with lust.

"Well, I hope it was as good for you as it was for me," Kevin said as he kissed me back. "That was one of the most incredible things I've ever experienced."

The musky smell of sex lingered in the room; as I stepped back, I rubbed my fanny with my hand and said, "Pooh, it smells like the fish quay on a sunny afternoon," as I looked at the white sticky stuff on my hand. I felt something dribbling down my right leg and looked at my fanny, which had stopped farting now; the golden mound and thick pink lips were dripping Kevin's spunk down my thigh.

"Using Hook Nose's sayings now, are we, making remarks about my fanny smelling?" Shelta, as Kevin, said, pointing to her real body.

"Time for a shower to get the niff off," I said, pulling his hand and guiding him to the bathroom.

Scratch scratch, woof woof, I heard as I opened the bedroom door; Ziggy was awake. She ran forward to greet what she thought was me and stopped. Her face registered bewilderment, and she growled. I put my hand down (as Shelta) and stroked her; she whimpered as if in pain.

"It's all right, beautiful," I said as I tickled behind her ear; she loved that. She seemed to recognise the tone of my voice and my actions but was totally confused.

"You go get a shower, and I'll try to explain to Ziggy what's happening," I said to Shelta as me.

The pup looked from side to side like someone watching a tennis match, first at me then at Shelta, backwards and forwards, making herself dizzy. Shelta in my body disappeared into the bathroom. The pup's eyes widened as I squatted down beside her. She couldn't understand that this gorgeous vision of femininity was using my tone of voice and mannerisms but wasn't me.

Use telepathy, she'll understand better, came Shelta's voice in my mind. I cupped her lovely little face with my two hands and caressed her neck as I looked into those huge brown eyes; this was something else only I did, and as I bent over and kissed her forehead, she knew it was me. What she couldn't understand was the long golden hair and the two tits bouncing against her face.

"Ziggy, it's me, darlin', Kevin," I said; she whimpered with confusion. "No, no; it's alright, sweet thing. Shelta and I have swapped places for a while."

Another whimper.

"She has my body with her mind, and I have her body with my mind."

She yapped excitedly as I stood up, showing her Shelta's magnificent body.

"Come on, little un," I said to her. "Time to see the pussies."

That was how I house-trained her when she was small, as she loved chasing cats (and still does). She bounded down the stairs, stopping now and then to see if I was following. She understood now that this beautiful vision floating down the stairs was really her master. I opened the back door to the garden, and she bounded out as she went to do her business. Totally unaware, I was standing there stark bollock naked as Shelta, my mind still not registering who I was with this mind mix thing. I head Ziggy barking like mad at my back door towards the neighbour's bedroom window. *Who is my back-door neighbour?* You ask yourself. Well, you couldn't mistake this person: Fuck Face Phillips stood there in all his glory.

Donkey knob rides again, I thought as he leered at Shelta's stunning vision, but not knowing it was me.

As Zig growled at his figure standing there, I said to her, "Payback time, baby; fancy some fun with Fuck Face?"

Ziggy hated him and loved to bite his ankles, so she ran round and round, jumping up and down with glee in answer to my request. *Strut your stuff, lady,* I said to myself as Derek's eyes started to bulge out of his head. I wasn't quite sure how to do this, act all girly girly, I mean, as I was still myself in my mind.

Don't worry; I'll help you, telepathised Shelta.

Believe me, Marilyn Monroe didn't have a look in, as Shelta's body did a Marilyn Monroe-type pose. I shook my hair wildly and bent down, tits swinging from side to side, showing my eyes, lifting my pouting face towards Fuck Face, and shaking my perfectly formed arse from side to side. I rose up to my full height and thrust out my wonderful full tits, nipples sticking out like sore thumbs. I parted those wonderful long legs wide to form a V shape, and my superb golden mound jutted out. Donkey knob started to rise. *Bloody hell,* I thought, *it's as big as a baby's arm.* I wonder if Shelta's body could take such a weapon.

I could take him in hairy and spit him our baldy, Kev, so don't worry, Shelta's voice said in my brain. *If you want to pay him back, I'm happy to help. I have an idea.*

Absolutely fucking brilliant, I telepathised back to her as my huge green eyes glared back at Fuck Face handling his weapon, pointing it at me like a loaded cannon.

I shook my head at him and pointed to his prick. *No, no*, I mouthed at him and closed my fist and started wanking it. *Thick bastard,* I thought to myself, so I used my finger and pointed at his prick and shook my head again. He stopped wanking, as I used my finger to thrust in and out my fist, removed it, pointed at his prick again, and then pointed at my cunt. I eased my finger down the hairs over the clitoris and into the lips and moved my finger up and down in the squelchy hole. Pooh, it stunk of fish; I really needed a shower. Derek's face was a treat as he finally got the message; he must have thought he had died and gone to heaven. As he looked back at me, I removed my finger from the hole and put it in my mouth, sucking it like a prick and then licking my tongue up and down in my mouth. He nodded his head up and down enthusiastically and drew a 69 on the window.

Finally, I thought as I nodded back, *payback time.* I made the shape of a telephone and pointed to Derek. As Zig and I walked back in the house, the phone rang.

"Hiya, sexy," Oozed out Fuck Face's la-de-dah voice. "Like what you saw? Dr Love's here to give you the meat injection."

What a fucking smarmy creep, I thought but said, in a sexy girly voice, "With something that size, it would probably bounce off my diaphragm."

"Tickle your tonsils, more like," came back Derek's quick retort.

"Well, big boy, why don't you give me a tonsillectomy, then? Kevin's going out soon, so watch for the car going, and then come through the gate in the back fence. I'll be waiting."

"What about the mad dog, though? It hates me and always bites me," whinged Derek.

"It's all right. Kevin's going to his mam's in Murton village, and he's taking Zig with him."

"Right, then; see you soon, gorgeous," and he put the phone down.

Shelta as me came into the living room and smiled. "You've got some lovely gear," she said, twirling round. "The aftershave and deodorant is excellent." She stood there as me in a beautiful black-and-white patterned shirt, wearing black high-waisted dress trousers with six pleats on either side and turn-ups on the bottom. The whole ensemble was completed by a pair of white leather loafers, a gold watch, and an amulet I got off George Hall, my mate. It was truly original, the sheikh of Oman's family crest, two crossed daggers with a palm tree on top; everyone admired it. I could smell the Joop aftershave wafting around the room.

"Couldn't have picked better myself," I said. "Boy, I'm a handsome bastard. By the way, don't you ever wear knickers or in this case underpants?" I looked down at the slight bulge sticking out the left side of my trousers.

"Hate the things," she replied. "Knickers and tights make me itch. Maybe a nice open-crotch G-string and stockings and suspenders, sometimes, but in this case, I want to feel your manhood. Right, give me the car keys, and I'll take Ziggy out for a walk. Then I'll get some shopping in."

Ziggy jumped up and down at the prospect of going out.

"I'll get some proper scampi and cook you a meal tonight after we change back."

"Change back," I echoed, gasping.

As I handed her the keys she replied, "Well, you don't want to stay like this forever do you?"

"No, no," I said, "but I've never had so much fun in all my life. I can't wait to pay back Fuck Face and the Snorting Dwarf."

"Okay, my little darlin'," she said, mimicking me perfectly. "After you finish with Derek, get showered and dressed, pick out some of my clothes, and I'll meet you at the Lodge at three."

I watched Shelta and the pup get in TBWSB and drive off, hoping Fuck Face was watching. Ten minutes later, I heard a tap on the back door; donkey knob had arrived, and it was payback time with a vengeance. *Why do I want so much revenge?* you ask. Well, with me working away so much, I didn't have time for women since Slut Bag (my ex-fiancée) and I split up. I did have women, as reps do when they're on the road, but I never took any women to the Lodge because of Fuck Face and the rest of them making rude remarks and groping them. So to get their own back, they put it round I was homosexual; nice, eh?

Okay, at the moment, I was in Shelta-Thari's body and loving every minute of it; it was a fabulous experience to be a woman for a while and experience what it felt like, but I wanted to be myself again. I enjoy being a man, but when they implied I was queer, it really hurt my manhood and pride. After walking into the bar with Shelta last night,, that would certainly quash the rumours, but I still wanted revenge and was about to get it as I opened the door.

Looking all shy and coy and acting all girly, I said to Fuck Face, "Upstairs quick, and lick me out while I suck your huge prick."

Four strides later, he was at the bedroom door, pulling his clothes off in a frenzy, his prick rising as I swayed sexily up the stairs. I tweaked my nipple and stroked my pussy as I stepped onto the landing. *Whoops, I think he's going to artex my ceiling,* I thought as his prick throbbed up even bigger than before.

"Lie on the bed," I commanded, and like a dutiful puppy, Derek obeyed.

As he lay there, his prick jutted up like Whitley Bay Lighthouse. I put on a CD, *The Greatest Rock Album in the World Ever II*; "Won't Get Fooled Again" by the Who came on. The lyrics say, "We won't get fooled again, oh no"; little did Fuck Face know. I straddled him, my face facing his toes and my arse and wide-open wet fanny looming over his face. I could see his expression in the reflection of the mirror. His eyes gaped wide open, his jaw dropped, and he licked his lips in anticipation at the sight of my gorgeous cunt. The music swelled loud, and the rock beat pulsed in conjunction with Derek's huge cock. I stuck my wet cunt in his face and could feel his hot, fetid breath against the lips of my hole. I rubbed it up and down on his nose and mouth. I thought, *It must stink like a cod*, as Fuck Face pushed me forward towards his prick, parting the cheeks of my bum with his thumbs as he stuck his whole face in my elasticated pussy hole. He thrust his tongue in my hole, like a viper attacking; the smell obviously didn't bother him.

As he munched at my piss flaps, I thought, *Please forgive me, Shelta.* Just the thought of him touching her made me sick, so I felt I should apologise.

No need to apologise, she telepathised, *but please don't put his dick in my mouth and certainly don't let him fuck me.*

No way, darlin'. I feel sick, even though it's in my mind, but here comes payback time.

I grabbed his prick, digging the red nails in very hard; I think I used more of my strength than Shelta's. Fuck Face squealed like a stuffed pig but still continued to drool over my pussy. I did what Shelta had whispered to me before and clenched my bum muscles very hard, gripping my face and nose. He winced as I let go, and a huge fart erupted in his face. He spluttered, gasping, as a smell like rotten eggs wafted round the room with the music. I giggled uncontrollably as I wanked his huge dick with both hands. It was some size; he could have won the three-legged race on his own with it. It throbbed hard, so I knew he was about to come, but I wasn't going to let that happen. It was payback time. I clenched my arse again and felt my stomach gurgle and rumble.

"Whoops," I said. "It must have been something I ate last night."

He spluttered as he talked, as he was still munching away at my pussy; his tongue was right down on my clitoris as he said, "No problem, no problem."

I could feel the rumbling grow as I unclenched the cheeks of my arse. I muttered under my breath, "You shit on my head [Geordie for "using and abusing"], so I'll shit on yours."

As I looked in the mirror to see what was happening, a little rasp then a spluttering sound came out of my bum hole, Derek pulled his face away. Just as he did, there was a loud spluttering as I did a huge wet fart all over his face, neck, and chest.

"You dirty, dirty bitch," Derek snapped, slimy shit dripping off him everywhere.

I could hear Shelta laughing raucously in my mind as I said in my best little girl voice, looking ever so coy, fluttering my eyelashes at him, "Oh, Derek, I'm so sorry." In my mind, I thought, *Got ya, ya bastard.* "I'll go and get you a towel." I ran to the bathroom with tears in my eyes, from laughing so much. "Here," I said, handing him a flannel and a towel. "You'd better take this and go home and have a shower."

"Pooh, it fucking reeks in here," he said, wiping and drying himself at the same time. "I've heard the expression she was a shit fuck [useless lay] before, but I never took it literally," he muttered as he headed down the stairs to go home.

I really needed to shower now, I thought as I headed for the bathroom. I quickly washed all her soft bouncy, curvy, and sticky out bits and took particular care to wash the genitals. I dried off, headed for the bedroom, and got out her suitcase. *What to wear, what to wear,* I thought, giggling to myself as I looked at all her clothes. *A girl's so spoilt for choice.* That's it, a very tight bright red minidress sprung into view. It would show her figure off to perfection. As I looked in the mirror, I took off the shower cap, and that wonderful hair cascaded down my back. *Good choice, Kev,* I said to myself; the dress was stunning. It showed every curve and line on her body; it looked as though it had been sprayed on. Well, nearly done; no knickers or tights to put on but there was make-up. Shit, I've never put make-up on in my life. Shelta did her face so well, and I didn't want to muck it up.

Don't worry, I heard, and a spectral form of Shelta's face appeared before me. I laughed.

What you laughing at? She asked.

Well, you can't suck my prick this time, can you? I asked, lifting up the skirt and exposing her pubes (rude bits).

She laughed at the sight of her own lovely bits covered in hair and said, "Move over."

Things reversed, and my head was floating like a mask now, watching her as she deftly applied her make-up.

"That's part of the mind mix; we can both be in the same body at the same time. I want to do it later on with you."

"Be in my body with me? Why?"

"I want to feel what it's like when you practice your kung fu and kendo."

"No problem; we'll go down to the beach in the morning. By the way, where is my body at the moment?"

"In the Lodge, having a pint; the pup's asleep in the car, and the Snorting Dwarf is spitting blood over Satinda, a beautiful Asian girl who's just started there." She finished her make-up and asked, "How do I look, then?"

"Put me back in, and I'll tell you." We reversed again. "Perfect," I said, looking at the reflection, and as I put on the four-inch heels and grabbed my bag, I added, "See you in the Lodge in five minutes, if I can walk in these heels."

"Don't worry; it'll be okay," she said as her face disappeared.

I locked the doors and walked towards the Lodge, which was just round the next bend. It's quite a busy area where I live; there's a little shopping mall and car park and cinema in the same block, so people were milling all around. I felt like a model in *Vogue* magazine, walking down the road with feline grace.

God, you're magnificent, Shelta, I thought as people's heads turned to watch her swaying down the road.

It must be a wonderful feeling of a power for a beautiful woman, as all the men looked at her with sheer lust, wanting to get into her panties, and all the women glared with jealousy, thinking, *She's got everything, and look at me.* I swayed from side to side, accentuating the hips and bum even more.

"Suck that, you bitches," I said, as their eyes burned with pure envy.

I shook my hair all around to make it glisten in the sun, pouted my lips, and tilted my head up in the air, pointing my nose up to make me look more arrogant.

"How pet, are ya alrite ["Hello, love, are you all right?" in Geordie]?" a voice said beside me.

Trying to act the arrogant bitch (God, did it feel good), I hadn't noticed Hook Nose Homer sidle up beside me (or what he thought was Shelta). I now know what it's like to be letched at, and ladies, you have my sympathy. His vulture eyes peeped over the glasses resting on the end of his nose, and they burned through me as he undressed me in his mind. *He scanned every square inch of her body, the perv*, I thought. *Well, let's have some fun.* I put my arm through his to link it.

"Hi, Rick," I said in my sexiest voice as I thrust my right breast into his arm. He flinched as a long, hard nipple brushed against his bare arm. Shelta was five feet, ten in her bare feet, but with four inch heels on, she looked like an Amazonian, towering over Hook Nose, who was five foot, seven at most.

"My, you're bonnie lass," he said, nose pointing in the air like a Concorde in flight as we neared the pub.

He stood up straight and strode out like a soldier, assuming people thought he was some kind of sugar daddy. I stroked his arm as I linked it and thrust my breast harder against it so he could feel all that lovely flesh. The nipple stuck out even more with the friction, and I watched him literally tremble with excitement. I pulled him to a stop (*Time for some fun,* I thought) and shoved my hips and fanny right against his groin.

"Got a light?" I asked, using my sexiest film-star voice.

As he lit my cigarette, I could feel his flaccid prick trembling, so I pushed against it with my fanny, rubbing up and down.

His eyes nearly popped out their sockets as he said, "I bet you wouldn't like that as a wart on the end of your nose," and pushed his groin against me.

I gave him my cutest girly look and said back, "Don't flatter yourself; you're so small, you should have been born a girl."

His prick went limp immediately. I stood back and tickled my clitoris, which was just peeking out of my micro skirt (it was just like when I saw Shelta in the car park). Hook Nose salivated as he saw the mound glinting in the sun.

"Christ, I think my clit's bigger than your dick."

He stood there shocked and stunned, blushing furiously, as I flounced into the pub car park. Just before going into the foyer, I turned sideways to look at him, still standing there mumbling, "Fucking bitch, ya dirty slut," and other obscenities in broad Geordie.

As I went into the bar, he glared at me, so I blew him a kiss, made a fist, and moved it up and down at him, indicating he was a wanker. As soon as Ziggy saw me, she came running over, yapping and jumping about with joy.

"Hi, darlin'," I said, patting her. I saw Kev in the corner as I went over.

"Nice one," he said, making reference to what I had just done to Hook Nose, who had just entered the bar. He looked at me and then mumbled under his breath.

"Two Jack Daniels and a bag of beefy crisps for the pup, please," I said to Satinda, the new barmaid. "Hi, my name is K— [whoops, I nearly slipped up], sorry, I mean Shelta-Thari, and that's Kev." I pointed over to Kevin. I could see the Snorting Dwarf glaring at her with envy as she handed me the drinks and crisps. As soon as I opened the crisps, Ziggy came scooting over, and I put them on the floor. "And that's the one and only Ziggy," I said as she crunched her way through the packet.

Satinda looked over at her and said, "She's beautiful: gorgeous eyes and really cute."

"Come round and meet her, and get yourself a drink," I replied, taking the drinks over to Kev.

"Doreen, I'm taking a break, okay?" she said, in a statement rather than a request.

"Go fuck yourself," the Snorting Dwarf grunted (such a nice lady, isn't she?), walking off and muttering away to herself, "Fucking Paki bastard."

Satinda came towards us; she was a stunner. She was short, like Doreen (Snorter), but boy, was she stacked. The Asian beauty had long, dark hair; she was slim but nicely rounded, with huge doe eyes. I could feel my juices rising as I was getting a mental hard-on looking at her ample breasts, bulging and swaying as she bent down to pat the pup.

Hey you, I don't know whether to be worried or angry, telepathised Shelta.

Worried or angry? I repeated, puzzled. *Sorry, you've lost me.*

She smiled as she returned to her thoughts, *Worried that if you're looking at her as Shelta, you're turning me lesbian, or angry because you're getting a mental hard-on as Kevin.*

I'm going to have to learn how to put a mental guard up against you, I replied, *but don't worry, my little pickled onion. I'm only a man, and she is lovely, but you're the only one for me.*

She smiled a knowing smile back at me.

Satinda squealed with delight as she handed Zig a crisp, and she did her "Please, please, please" trick.

"Isn't that cute?" she said, looking at me and then Kevin.

I thought of another trick Ziggy did, which made me think of another way to get back at Hook Nose, who was looking at our group, shaking his head and muttering, "Bunch of fucking arseholes."

He was sitting at the bar, which was empty apart from ourselves. I put a crisp in my mouth, gripping just the tip with those luscious ruby red lips, and squatted down on the ground, my front facing Hook Nose. As he looked over, straight up my skirt (don't forget, Shelta never wore knickers), he spluttered his pint all over the bar as my tadger (fanny) peeked at him.

"Gently, baby," I said to the pup as she came over and very carefully took the crisps out of my mouth, kissing me at the same time. As Zig sat there, contentedly chewing her crisps, Shelta (as me) and Satinda laughed in amusement.

"Oh, she's just great," Satinda said as she stroked the pup. "I just love her."

"I know who would love you," I said, looking at her. "Our mate Micky. I'll just give him a ring."

I was still on my haunches, and Hook Nose, looking just like a vulture, was still staring between my legs, licking his lips in anticipation. I spread my loins wide apart and displayed all that lovely shagging tackle hanging there. As my glistening golden mound peeked at him, he started frantically rubbing the front of his trousers.

I hope you realise people are going to call me a right bitch after this, Kevin D'Arcy, she telepathised.

Just getting my own back; payback time, remember? He was another one who slagged me off. I knew what Hook Nose was going to do, and I said, "Watch this," as he jumped up and ran to the toilet.

"Just going to the loo," said Shelta as me.

Satinda looked up, oblivious to what had been going on, as she was stroking Zig, who was lying on her back, very contented.

I stood up and said, "I'll just go and ring Micky, Satinda; back in a minute."

Mental Micky answered the phone, and I said, "Hi, Mick, its Kev [whoops, don't forget your Shelta-Thari at the moment] … Kev's girlfriend Shelta. We're in the Lodge; come over, we've got someone special we'd like you to meet.

"Okay, sweetheart," he replied. "Be over in five minutes."

Satinda looked doubtful and said, "I hope he's nice."

"You'll love him," I replied. "You two will get on like a house on fire." Kevin came back in the bar laughing loudly. "Something funny?" I asked.

Shelta as Kevin was laughing so much, she could barely talk but said, "Please forgive me for being rude, Satinda, but Hook Nose is beating his meat in the toilet; the slapping and moaning is echoing round the toilet. Half of West Monkseaton must be able to hear him."

"They're all a bunch of wankers in here, excluding you two, of course," Satinda replied, glaring at the Snorting Dwarf, who was dying to find out what we were laughing at. The pup joined in with us laughing as she jumped up and down, yapping away merrily.

In my mind, Shelta said, *What a strange feeling it was in the toilet, having to stand up and aim your prick to piss.*

I know. When I went for a piss this morning, I put my hand down to hold it, forgetting I was you. But what about Hook Nose wanking? My trick worked, didn't it? I hope he has his magnifying glass and tweezers with him while he's wanking because when I pushed against him this morning, it was tiny.

If you were a real woman, you would be a first-class slut; do you know that?

Well, I replied, *I'm only going to be a woman once, so I want to make the most of it.*

Not quite, Kev; I want to show you something else tomorrow.

Don't ask; you'll find out, I retorted as she smiled at me, pre-empting what she was going to say.

Mental Micky walked in and saw the three of us laughing in the corner. As he smiled and waved at us, the Humpy-Backed Git, Ron Turner, came in shuffling and twitching. Every village has its village idiot, and he was it. As I looked at this pathetic excuse for a man through Shelta's gorgeous eyes, I thought how unkind nature was to certain human beings. He was the same age as me (as Kevin), but that's where the resemblance ended. We had both gone to the same school together; the poor bastard had always looked the same. He was older and uglier, if this was possible. His mane of sandy hair was fairly long and wavy, very thick and wiry. His sideburns and ears sprouted hairs all over the place, as his face did Albert Steptoe contortions, twitching away. He always wore a shirt and tie and some sort of jacket and trousers; today, he wore a suit.

Ron was fairly well off, as he was paid off from the Ministry of Defence on sick grounds. All he did was drink all day and have wet dreams over Fiona Leeming, the girl from Middle Wallop I had brought back with us. They had once been an item, but he pestered her so much, she had to move away. Obviously, he was the butt of everyone's jokes, like, "Don't upset him or you'll get his back up. He's got loads of money; it was his back pay"; you know the sort of thing.

I watched him and Doreen talking as she got him a pint. He slopped most of it as his twitching hand lifted it to his mouth.

Shelta's voice said, *Jesus Christ, can you imagine them two having sex and conceiving a baby?* I shuddered at the thought of a Snorting Humpy-Backed Git Dwarf.

I take it you can't stand those two; well, neither can I, so how about some more payback time? Shelta thought, as I turned round to see her looking out the window.

I could feel the lust oozing out of the Humpy-Backed Git as he watched me walk over to Kevin. Snorter was glaring daggers at me as I asked Shelta what she was up to. Mental Micky and Satinda were talking away sixty to the dozen, with Ziggy lying asleep on Satinda's knees. I knew they would hit it off, and I was right. I followed Kevin's eyes and looked out at the car park. At first, I didn't see what he was pointing at, but then I saw Sharon (Slut Bag), my ex fiancée, flouncing across the car park, fucking arrogant bitch. Then I saw what I was supposed to: two dogs humping the arses off each other. One was a scraggy Yorkshire terrier, and the other one was a large sandy-coloured cross-breed, wire-haired thing. The small one, the bitch, was pinned down by the big one, who was too big for her tadger, so he just whopped it up the nearest hole: her poor bum.

Poor little soul, I thought as I looked at her. Ziggy wouldn't let anyone near her pride and joy; she would have ripped his throat out. She looked at me from Satinda's lap, as if she had heard my thoughts (she had, as she was now part of the matrix), and gave a little growl, as if to say, "Yes, you're right."

Clicked on yet? It struck me like a thunderbolt. I stared at the two dogs and then looked back at the Snorting Dwarf and the Humpy-Backed Git.

Oh no, I said as Shelta's eyes widened and her mouth gaped in mute horror. *You wouldn't,* I said, looking at Kevin.

Mind mix time, Shelta's voice said in my head, using my real body's lips. It was done in a second, and it was mayhem.

The two figures of Snorter and Humpy ran round like wild things, as they exchanged minds with the dogs. The two dogs shuddered as the transference was completed. The two dogs in Snorter and Humpy's minds went wild in their bodies. I don't know dog language, but you can picture how they felt. As the two of them ran round the bar, staring with wild eyes and making funny noises, they collided heavily with Slut Bag, who had just walked in the door, sending all her bags and herself to the floor. But the best bit was, it knocked her wig off, showing her bald, stubbly, scarred head (I'll explain later). She patted the top of her head and screamed her face a grimace of embarrassment.

"You brain-dead, stupid, subhuman fucking pigs," she cried.

I laughed so much; the tears were running down my face, smudging all the make-up. My jaw was aching and so were my sides, which were nearly splitting in two. *God, tits don't half get in the way,* I thought as I tried to hold myself together.

My body of Kevin just stood there with a mischievous grin spread across its face, eyes gleaming with delight. I could feel my fanny starting to dribble as I clasped my hand to it. I watched Slut Bag disappear into the ladies, and as I ran towards the door, I head Micky and Satinda laughing raucously, the puppy barking madly as she ran around in circles after the Humpy-Backed Git and the Snorting Dwarf's bodies, probably sensing the dog presence.

"Got to go to the loo," I shouted, both hands grasping her fanny, which was dribbling down my thigh. When I opened the toilet door, I saw Slut Bag feverishly trying to put her wig on straight.

I heard Hook Nose in his usual eloquent style shouting, "Come in here for a quiet drink, and I'm surrounded by barmy bastards; go on, fuck off, the lot of ya, crazy fuckers."

The Slut (for short) eyed me up and down as my beautiful body blazed past her to the loo. I just made it as I sat down and my pee gushed out, splattering the bowl hard. The relief was enormous, and as I sat drying myself, I decided to have some fun with the Slut. I opened my handbag and sprayed on some femme fresh.

Don't want a smelly one in here, do we?

Thanks for being so considerate, telepathised Shelta.

You're welcome, I replied back.

I opened the toilet door, and the Slut could see my stunning vision reflecting back at her. This bitch hated any good-looking women, especially ones with nice tits and beautiful figures. She made my life hell when I lived with her; she was insanely jealous. My bag clattered as I took out the make-up bag and started to repair my face. I did it myself, with no help from Shelta, and got a strange feeling that the longer your mind stayed in someone else's body in a mind mix, the more like them you become.

That's very true, Kevin; that's very perceptive of you. I'll explain later, Shelta's voice said, entering my mind again as I finished my face.

God, you're gorgeous, I thought as I brushed my long gleaming hair very slowly in front of the Slut, who was applying some kind of glue to her scarred dome of a head. As I smoothed my dress down back into shape, I languished over every curve on my body, again for spite, as I knew she'd be seething with jealousy. She glared at me with maliciousness in her eyes, and I gave her one of my (well, Shelta's) heart-melting smiles, white teeth gleaming. Her eyes spat out hate as I looked back in the mirror, thinking of Beauty and the Beast.

She was no Beast when I first met her ten years ago; in fact, she was a lot like Shelta at the time. She was tall and slim, with long blonde hair and large blue eyes; not much for tits, but a nice round figure, and an amazingly tight pussy. To sum her up, she always said that she looked like Clodagh Rodgers, a singer from years ago, and she did a bit. After we split, it was bad, woman scorned and that type of thing. I won't go into graphic details, as we all know what that's like. Suffice to say, she did me a favour, as I am where I am because of her.

She was (and still is) a nurse, not far from where I live, so I just wanted to get well away from her and all the trouble she was causing. I was a salesman in a shop at the time and was very depressed one night, so I went on the piss and bumped into James Rowan (JR, or Seven Bellies). We got on great, and he had just fired a sales representative, so he offered me a job. I hate the fat bastard, but I'll always be grateful for that job, as it got me away from the Slut and all her trouble. It was an amazing feeling not having to look over my shoulder all the time (yes, things were that bad), waiting to see what she would do next. Anyway, I became JR's top salesman, bought another house and car, forgot about her, and went on with my life. It was only when I came home I felt anxious again. Normally, she wasn't in the Lodge at the weekend, so I could relax, but she did come in mid-week for drinks, and since this was Wednesday, here she was, not that she would recognise me looking like this.

Well, how did she become a Beast? You ask. I was so depressed at the time of the break-up, as she had stitched me up with the police and lost me a manager's job. I was on the dole, so I took three hundred paracetamols and slit my wrist. I woke up three and a half hours later, farted, burped, and then spewed. My wrist was clogged up with matted blood, but I was alive, so I thought, *You're not wanted by God*, yet so I started my life afresh.

I really wanted her dead (the Slut, that is), and I could have killed her in a million ways with the martial arts I know, but I didn't. A wise woman once told me, "God pays back without taking money." By not doing anything to her, the Hierarchy decided to pay her back for all the nasty, evil things she did to me. They made her have a cerebral aneurism, and she nearly died. Her daughter (not mine) found her slumped on the floor; they rushed her to the hospital and operated on her just in time. The baldness and scars were from the operation; her hair did not grow back properly. Her once-lithe figure had swelled with all the drugs and steroids she had to take. So with her cheap NHS wig and disfigured head, her plump body and face, she became the Slut Bag or the Beast, as I was now describing her. The long hours and the vodka hasn't helped much, either, as the booze had discoloured the once-blue eyes and peachy complexion, and her job had made her bad-tempered and grumpy. So God does pay back without taking money, doesn't he?

As she tried to tidy up her frumpish face and clothes, I took a little brush with very soft bristles out of my bag; the Slut's eyes narrowed as she watched me lift up the front of my skirt to expose Shelta's pride and joy. I started brushing the lovely golden curls, exposing those luscious, pink piss flaps. Slut Bag's eyes popped with mute disbelief as I licked my finger, put it right on my clitoris, and rubbed it. As it jumped to attention, I shivered, fluttered my eyelids, and pouted my lips as its top peeped out.

"Us girls have got to keep the mutton button in good order," I said, grinning from ear to ear. "I've got to keep it looking good and feeling good for my fiancé, Kevin. Kevin D'Arcy, do you know him, by the way?"

If looks could kill, Shelta would have got the death of a thousand cuts by the way she glared at her.

"Course I do, the fucking arsehole. He and I lived together for six years. You're just the kind of slut I knew he'd end up with, so go fuck yourself."

Move over, Kevin, I heard Shelta say in my mind as she took over her body with me still inside.

Whoops! The Slut Bag shouldn't have said that, I thought, as our minds merged inside her body. Shelta's eyes blazed blue as she held Slut Bag in her hypnotising gaze. Like a puppet, the Slut stared back, her idiotic face blank as she squatted down, legs wide apart, sitting on her haunches. Her fanny was wide open, dripping vaginal juices in a little puddle on the floor, her piss flaps also open, thick and juicy, pushing out of her thick pubic hair.

"Go fuck yourself, bitch," Shelta spat out with venom I'd never heard nor ever wanted to hear again, as she handed the Slut Bag the brush I had been using earlier. She grabbed it eagerly, eyes rolling and mouth slobbering, as she rammed it, handle first, into her now bubbling hole. She rammed it up and down with furious movements as it rubbed against her fully extended clitoris. She held onto the sink with her left hand for support as she masturbated furiously with the brush. Her head held back, he wig tilting on one ear as her right hand rammed in and out, screaming herself into an orgasmic frenzy.

God, she'll not piss for a week if she carries on like that, I thought, tears streaming down my face, as Shelta telepathised, *Well, I'm going to your body now; enjoy payback time, Kevin*, as she slid back to my form in the bar. Just as she disappeared, the Snorting Dwarf barged through the toilet door, rubbing the cheeks of her arse; an acrid smell floated round. Her arse was squelching with diarrhoea, the same time as the Slut's fanny was squelching her cum as she orgasmed, bobbing up and down, screaming in ecstasy, as she fell to the floor, looking like a dead sparrow with its legs in the air. She lay there gasping, her passion spent.

As I opened the door to go back to the bar, I heard Snorter muttering as she wiped her arse.

"God, me arsehole hurts. It feels as though I've had something rammed up it."

If you only knew, I thought as I entered the bar, or did she? The first thing I saw was the Humpy-Backed Git with Ziggy yapping round his legs, staring at the front of his trousers, where an ever growing wet patch appeared.

"Bastard, bastard, I've come in me pants," he mumbled, shuffling backwards and forwards as Ziggy snapped at his ankles. Kevin, Satinda, and Micky were sitting at the table, doubled up with laughter as I walked over and sat down, the pup jumping up beside me. As we talked, the smell hit me first, then the Cumbrian voice. There's only one thing on earth that smells like that, and I'd know that voice anywhere: Wurzel and Seven Bellies had arrived. As everyone's eyes watered and noses wrinkled with the smell, Les Kent (Wurzel) just stood there, grinning with delight. He seemed to take some sadistic pleasure in knowing he smelt like dog shit on someone's foot.

"Well now, Kev," Seven Bellies said in his Geordie/Cumbrian drawl, "you've had a good week, haven't you?" He smiled his nearly toothless grin and asked, "Now where's the fucking cash?"

Shelta as me just smiled, as she stood straight up, towering over him, shoving my ample breasts in his face, nearly in his mouth as I bent over him.

"Now, now you horribly fat little thing, that's not very nice in front of ladies, is it?" I said, huge green eyes glaring at his piggy slits.

He could hardly talk as his lips trembled against my breasts but managed to splutter out, “Oh, I am terribly sorry, my dear, but that’s just me; no offence meant. I do apologise,” in his best posh voice, which he thought impressed people.

“Well, sit down and talk properly then, and if you can’t say anything nice, don’t say anything at all, okay?” I pouted at him, doing my very best Shelta impression.

“Yes, yes, okay. Sorry. I’ll get the drinks in then, shall I, while you get all that lovely money then, Kev.”

“Okay,” I said, “but before I do, please remove that obnoxious odour.” I looked at Wurzel. The smell was getting worse, as Wurzel secreted out even more horrible smells.

“Someone open the fucking windows,” Hook Nose said, in fine form, for once. “Somebody’s shit themselves.” I had to agree with him.

Mental Micky stood up and opened the fire exit door, which led onto the Main Street. Satinda came from behind the bar and walked over to Micky, gulping in fresh air, like we all were to rid ourselves of the shitty taste and smell of Wurzel.

She said something to Micky, who came over and said, “Look, Shelta, its five o’clock, and Satinda’s finished, so we’re going over to my place for a bite to eat. While you and Kev are talking business, we’ll take Ziggy over to give you some peace.”

At the mention of her name, the pup jumped up, yapping with delight; she ran over to Micky and Satinda.

As Kev came through the door, I could hear TBWSB’s alarms resetting, and I said to Micky, more as Shelta than me, “Thank you, Micky. You’re a darling; isn’t he, Kev? He wants to take Zig for a walk with Satinda while we talk with JR.”

"Fine by me," replied Kev as Seven Bellies grinned from ear to ear at the mention of JR (well, I couldn't call him Seven Bellies in public, could I?).

"Wurzel, f— [He nearly said "fuck" again, as my green eyes flashed at him.] Find yourself a seat elsewhere and get yourself a drink while Kevin and I and this lovely lady talk."

Wurzel walked off, muttering to himself, as I gave him my best girly smile and said, in a Marilyn Monroe voice, "Thank you, Mr Rowan. That's very kind of you."

"You're welcome," he said, smiling back, but he had positioned himself to look straight up Shelta's skirt to see her glorious pussy.

I immediately felt horny, and my pussy started to ache; it wanted to be licked, sucked, caressed, and made love to. My eyes widened in disbelief as Rowan watched my love lips expand and get moist. If I had had knickers on, I would have come in them. Kev smiled at Seven Bellies and then me, panic registering on my face as I thought, *Fuck me, I'm getting horny over that fat ugly bastard looking at my tadger.* My nipples were rapidly pushing the fabric of the dress out, and I could feel them fully erect as the friction of the cloth rubbed against them. I saw JR's trousers bulge and thought, *God; I must be turning queer if I'm getting turned on by him looking at me.*

Don't worry, handsome; it's me doing it, Shelta telepathised. My eyes fluttered, and I breathed a sigh of relief as she added, *Time to change back to ourselves now. I told you, the longer you stay in a body, it starts to take over. I started to get horny as you; your trousers were about to burst as I looked at myself, all girly and pouting, so I am transferring us back over. It's really me, transferring my hormones from one body to another.*

Flash! I was back in my body, with my own mind. My groin ached as I looked back at Shelta, fluttering her eyelids, pouting her mouth, licking her ruby red lips, and staring at me. *Poor fat bastard; if he only knew*, I thought as he continued to stare at Shelta's piece of heaven.

Gorgeous George came in the bar door, and I said, "Excuse me, George. I need a favour." He came over, and I explained that Seven Bellies and I had a lot of money that needed to be counted in private.

"No problem," George said. "Of course you can use my office."

He led us up to his office. Both Shelta and I looked across the bar, where the Snorting Dwarf, the Humpy-Backed Git, Wurzel, and the Slut Bag were getting on famously. Snorter was rubbing her arse, still muttering; Humpy was looking at the white stain of his trousers, pointing at it while shaking his head at Snorter. Wurzel and the Slut were all over each other like a rash. She loving the attention whilst he licked his lips and held her hand, muttering sweet nothings in her ear in anticipation of fucking something more than his fist. The four of them glared at me and then Shelta as I passed them by. As the Slut stood up to go to the bar, I noticed she was walking bow-legged, a grimace on her face as her bum jutted out. *Her fanny must be killing her*, I thought as she waddled over.

She threw daggers at me with her eyes as I walked past, so I turned and said in a mocking tone, "I've heard of brushing up on a subject before but never brushing up on a cunt. Enjoy it, did we?"

The mute horror registered on her face as she looked back at me as if to say, "How the fuck did you know?" She looked at Shelta and then me, eyes blazing.

I could still feel the daggers in my back from her gaze as I heard Shelta's voice in my head say, *You were wrong, Kev; she's so sore, she won't piss for two weeks, and Wurzel hasn't got a hope in hell of getting laid.*

I burst out laughing, and JR asked, "Something funny, Kevin?" in his smarmy Cumbrian voice.

"Just laughing about something Shelta-Thari and I did today," I said.

"Must have been good," he said.

"Oh, it was," I replied, still laughing as we went into the office to get the business out of the way.

After counting the money and stashing it in his briefcase, JR said goodbye and walked to the car park, giggling to himself and rubbing his hands at the thought of all that lovely money.

As he got in his Jaguar XJ6, he said, "Tell the smelly bastard to make his own way home. I'm going straight to the bank with the money, and I'll have to get some air freshener or something because the car stinks." He drove off, still frowning.

"Bye, Jim," I said, waving into his rearview mirror and went back into the bar.

It was fun to be Shelta-Thari, but I was glad I was me again, as I used my very muscular legs to stride into the bar. I turned right, but there was no Wurzel or the Slut. I turned right towards Shelta, who was just dozing off in the corner. My prick hardened as I looked at her gorgeous body languishing on the chair, her legs slightly apart as she slid down to get more comfortable, exposing thigh and pubes.

God, I love you, I said to myself.

I noticed Wurzel; well, smelt him first, as he and Slut Bag waddled around the corner. She was waddling like she had rickets as Wurzel guided her to the bar phone.

In his very la de dah voice, he said, “Taxi for Kent in the Hunting Lodge Bar down to Potter Bank, as soon as possible. Five minutes? That’s fine.”

Potter Bank? You’ve come down in the world, I thought as I watched them on their bar stools sitting patiently for their taxi.

I sat next to Shelta and gently stroked the delicate features of her face; her eyelids fluttered open.

“Hello, beautiful,” I said, my voice full of love for this amazing woman the gods had deemed to give me.

As her eyes refocused, she wearily said, “I told you what is borrowed must be returned, Kevin. I’m sorry, but it’s really taken it out of me. How do you feel?”

Well, I’m lucky, as I self-generate my powers straight away, so I felt great, but I stifled a pretend yawn and said, “Yeah, I’m tired as well. Let’s go to bed, but just to sleep.”

“You’re a liar, Kevin D’Arcy,” she replied, “but I love you for it; thank you.”

She then stood up, pressed all her lovely feminine bits against me, and kissed me passionately on the lips. My whole body flooded with warmth as our lips embraced. We stopped, and our eyes locked; we both got whacked at the same time.

We both shuddered, and Shelta said, “Kevin, I’m pregnant. I’ve just been told by Taliesin.”

Our eyes still locked, her eyes filling with tears of joy, mine with just tears, the jukebox started to play "The Man with the Child in His Eyes"; my whole body portrayed every emotion known to a human being: joy, happiness, pride, you name it, as I listened to Kate Bush sing those wonderful words.

"He's some joker, that Taliesin," I said to Shelta, my eyes still sparkling with tears. "God, I want to tell the whole world about this: my mam, my sisters, aunties, uncles, nieces, nephews, friends, the lot. Let's get Ziggy and tell Micky and Satinda, then go home, and I'll ring everyone."

"Ziggy already knows," she said. "I was mind mixing with her when you thought I was asleep before. So do Micky and Satinda, as they have become one with each other. All three have a very special part to play in this. Ziggy will save our lives; she's a very special little lady. I think you know she's been here before."

I shuddered with the realisation of what she had just said. I had often jokingly said, as I looked into those deep brown eyes, "You've been here before, little 'un." I thought I recognised something. It now hit me: Edith Anne, my nanna.

"Micky and Satinda are also very special," she continued. "Micky is quite psychic but doesn't know how to use it yet. He will be trained. Satinda has lots of mystical powers, and she does know it; we will need their help. This baby is very special, Kevin. It's a child of the matrix, the first one for five hundred years. Remember when I started bleeding in Amesbury and I was startled? Well, this is the first."

"What about you, though? You have the gift; isn't Iuatha your mother?"

"No, Kevin, you're wrong. I'm sorry, but I couldn't tell you till I was sure."

Pain hit me, and I was confused as I asked, "Who are your mother and father, then?"

"Iuatha was taken from the de la Wyle family, as she was good, unlike Toutaitis. She became my guardian, my surrogate mother.

Still confused, I replied, "And your father, Lugus; is he your guardian also?"

"Yes," she said very quietly. "My father is Taliesin, lord of the matrix; he is both my mother and father, as he is a hermaphrodite, as our child will be."

Bewilderment hit me as I fell into the chair, dazed.

A taxi outside honked its horn, and the Slut and Wurzel walked off, giving us dirty looks as they went.

"Fuck you," I said, black angry eyes staring back, and I shuddered.

My eyes narrowed into black slits as it hit them. Shock waves rippled through them as I went into a trance and vented all my anger at them. They had both bent down to get in the taxi, their arses sticking up in the air, when their bums exploded with shit. Wurzel's underpants and trousers strained as a huge lump of shit pushed its way against the cloth. Slut Bag's knickers and skirt did the same.

I turned, looking like a male version of Sissy Spacek in Stephen King's *Carrie,* and directed my gaze at a laughing Hook Nose Homer, sitting on the bar stool. He shuddered, and his pint started spilling as his pants filled with a huge shit, lifting him off the stool. Shelta was aghast as I turned on Snorter and Humpy; the same thing happened to them, and they stopped laughing. Fuck Face Phillips peeked his head round the door, looking for George to see if he was still barred, when his gaze hit mine. As he lifted his arrogant nose in the air, the same thing happened to him. He hobbled to the bar, grunting as the strain hit him, his pants inched out bit by bit as he moved to the counter, hands gripping it. All hell broke loose. The shit was spraying everywhere; if there had been a fan, it would have hit it.

The taxi driver waved angrily at the Slut and Wurzel and told them, "Fuck off, you dirty bastards; you're not stinking my cab out," as he drove off, leaving them behind.

Snorter, Humpy, Hook Nose, and Fuck Face let out deep group groans as the huge lumps came to an end. There were loud rasping, farting, and squelching noises as the shit came out and flattened, and then ran down their legs. George came into the bar, wondering what all the noise was, and then he sniffed the air.

"Pooh, some dirty bugger's dropped his bait," he said. "It stinks in here."

Slut Bag and Wurzel ran to the toilets, mumbling, "How we going to get home now?"

Snorter grabbed her arse and said, "Oh, fuck, not again."

Humpy just looked at the spunk stain on the front of his trousers as he patted the shit stains on the back. "I'll have to buy some new trousers now," he said as he shuffled about.

"Bastards, bastards, bastards," groaned Hook Nose, as he sped out the door to go home. Gorgeous George stared at Fuck Face, ready to tell him he was barred from last night's episode, when Derek's eyes looked pleadingly at me and Shelta. I just glared at him.

As the stink rose all around, he looked at George's open mouth and wandered off, saying, "This has got to be one of the shittiest days I've ever had. First her [he looked at Shelta], and now this [he looked at me]."

As he disappeared out of the bar, a blue aura was round Shelta as I looked at her. *Just protecting myself,* she telepathised.

My eyes returned to normal as we got up to leave. “They are all a load of shit, and now they know it,” I said, taking her hand and leading her towards the car.

As I disarmed TBWSB, I saw Gorgeous George standing in the bar. When I looked through the French windows, he was sniffing the air and spraying a can of air freshener as he shook his head in bewilderment at what he had just witnessed. I burst out laughing, and so did Shelta, as we drove off.

After we pulled into my driveway, I armed the car, and we walked to the front door.

Shelta said, “I told you you’d get stronger” (meaning the power of the matrix).

“I don’t know what happened; all I thought was, ‘You’re all a load of shit,’ and all hell broke loose. They deserved it, anyways.”

“Until you gain control, Kevin, you must be careful,” she said in a serious tone. “You could have killed them.” I gasped at that thought and looked at her with pleading eyes. “Don’t worry, I’ll explain it all on the beach tomorrow. You said you wanted to watch the sunrise. Let’s forget about the scampi [I laughed], the real scampi, and get some rest. We’ll need it.”

Deep thunder rumbled in the distance.

Another bad omen, I thought as I headed up to the bedroom. I rang Micky and told him the good news and explained what had happened in the bar, and then I asked him if he could keep Ziggy till morning. He said she was asleep in the basket in the garage, and I could call her and she’d come out of the dog flap in the garage door. I said goodnight and looked at the love of my life, already fast asleep. She was so drained; she hadn't even taken her clothes off. She lay curled up like a foetus. She looked so sweet, young, and innocent as she lay there, but this vision of loveliness was deadly.

She was a high priestess of the Sidhe race, after all, and as I lay down beside her, I wondered what fate would befall us. What about the baby? My mind was a whirl as I drifted off to sleep. Who would give her away for the wedding? Should I call Taliesin or, as she had just told me, Dad?

A deep baritone voice said quietly in my mind, *Don't worry, my son; she has already been given away, and yes, you can call me Dad.*

Thanks, Dad, I replied and went into oblivion.

Chapter 11

Beware the Ratapa and the Broichan Sacrifice to Artemis

The hi-fi switched itself on at 3 a.m. exactly, and some silly early-morning music awoke me with a start. I jumped up and grabbed my balls and chest. *Thank God for that: no tits, no fanny*, I thought, sighing with relief. I turned as Shelta shook herself awake; just I had done as her yesterday.

“Morning, handsome.”

“Morning, my little darling; well, little darlings,” I replied as I patted her stomach. My hand lingered on her belly, and she put her two hands on top of mine. The effect was instantaneous; I jumped.

“Whoa, it’s only a few days old, and I can feel it already,” I said as my right hand throbbed with pins and needles.

“I told you, it’s no ordinary baby. It isn’t a freak of nature; she’ll be born with your colouring, dark and tanned, and your strength. But she will be a clone of me in every other way: facially, bodily, and all my powers.”

“That’s some baby,” I said. “A girl. A baby girl. But where does the hermaphrodite come in? Is it part man and woman?”

“No, no, that’s why we need to talk. She can be both.”

I jumped out of bed and replied, “Get dressed; I’ll make a flask of coffee and get the stuff ready. Then you can tell me on the beach.”

Downstairs, as the kettle boiled, I heard her banging around. Five minutes later, she appeared, draped across the doorframe. She wore a black cat suit which accentuated every contour and every line of her glorious figure. She also wore a small nylon bomber jacket and black sandals. Her tadger stuck out the front like a baby's bum, and her breasts and nipples strained against the fabric of the cat suit. Even at three in the morning, she was a stunner. I could see the hairy mound pushing against the fabric, and the cleft of her pussy left an indent in it. As she posed from side to side of the frame, every part of her moved; I did too. The one-eyed milkman jutted out as I watched her, and the fabric of my dressing gown rose.

"Oh," she said, eyes growing wide. "I see someone's glad to see me." She stroked my shaft.

"Let's pick up the pup and get down to the beach first, and I can have a work out to get rid of the stiffness."

She bent down and swallowed half my cock; after she pulled it out she said, "I'll get rid of it now, if you want."

Groin aching, I replied, "Please, love of my life, and wait. Put the stuff in the car, and we'll do it later."

Giving me a pouty look, she said, "Okay; hurry up, and I'll start the car."

I dashed upstairs to get ready and thought, *Shit, if she presses the wrong button, she'll wake up the whole neighbourhood.*

The boot opened, and Shelta put in the bag with the coffee, croissants, dog food, biscuits, and plates. She wrapped the blanket around Asmodeus (the samurai sword) and laid it beside them. I looked out the window and smiled.

It's okay, Kev, she thought. *I read your mind and used the silent mode on the alarm.*

I waved back an acknowledgement as she slid in the driver's seat. TBWSB purred as she switched her on. All ready, I locked the front door of the house and jumped in the passenger seat behind her. She drove with great skill; TBWSB seemed to like her. We reached Micky's, and out popped a little head, ears cocked. I knew Ziggy would hear the car. She ran and jumped straight into the car, licking me and Shelta, jumping from one to another.

Shelta drove off, and the pup settled down on my knee. Whitley Bay was only a mile and a half away; we turned down Monkseaton Drive and went straight down to the Links. As we turned left at the bottom onto the Links, Whitley Bay Lighthouse loomed up like a huge white monolith to our right, light flashing as we watched it. The beach and island looked magnificent, silhouetted by a red and gold sky; it was breathtaking. We pulled to a stop at the cove just before the lighthouse and parked on top of the small cliff. The three of us got out the car, and the pup ran down the pathway to the cove, bouncing up and down like a spring lamb, barking as she went. Shelta locked the car after I took all the gear out, and we cuddled each other as we looked out over the bay.

"Kevin, it's magnificent," she said. "It's like being on a different planet. I now see why you love it at this time of the day."

I breathed deeply and took in that wonderful fresh salty air, and as I breathed out, relaxing my muscles at the same time, I replied, "This is my little piece of heaven."

I took her hand and led her to the beach. The water looked blue/black, like ink, as we stepped onto the sand, where Ziggy was rolling about. We stretched out the blanket on the beach about ten feet away from the water, and Ziggy jumped straight on it, yapping as she did so.

"She wants her breakfast," I said to Shelta as I put down her dish and filled it with nice morsels and biscuits.

Ziggy munched away contentedly as I poured us a coffee and handed one to Shelta. The caffeine kicked in as soon as it hit my stomach, and a warm glow spread through me. Shelta smiled at me as the same thing happened to her. I pointed north just past the lighthouse, and on the horizon rose the gigantic figure of the Blyth Power Station, steaming away.

"That's the power station there," I said, and she looked to see where I was pointing.

"It's enormous, isn't it?" she replied.

"It heats the sea up for miles so you get huge basking sharks around the area, but they're harmless," I stated as she shuddered at the thought.

I stood up, breathed deeply, and then tested all my muscles. I let out a low groan as I held a pose for ten seconds and then let out my breath and relaxed my muscles.

Shelta jumped as I did a quick karate punch and shouted, "Ah ya!" I planted the heel of my right foot in the ground and twisted it, screaming, "Agh-h-h-h!" I gave her my best Bruce Lee look, and she tottered back in surprise. "I bet that scared you," I said, bowing at her like you do after a martial arts bout.

"Just a bit; you scared the hell out of me. You have such a wild streak inside you, Kevin."

I touched her shoulder gently, looked at her confused face, and said, "I'm a lover, not a fighter, my darling. I only hurt people who hurt me or others. You know I love children, animals, and old people; it's just the rest I can't get on with."

"You're a complete nutter, you know that, Kevin D'Arcy, but inside, you're a very deep and serious man."

"I love you too, sweetheart," I replied, teasing her.

"Please, Kevin," she implored. "Try to understand: You are now part of the matrix; we are as one now. You can unleash terrible power if you wish; that's what I was trying to tell you yesterday when you whacked Humpy and them. You could have killed them."

My heart leapt with fear. I wasn't joking now as I stuttered out, "H-h-how?"

"When you use telekinesis, mind scanning, or anything like that, like in *Scanners, Carrie,* or *The Fury,* you see them bleed, their bodies blow up, that sort of thing. Well, you can unleash that power."

My mind reeled with this awesome discovery. She smiled a very loving, gentle smile full of concern.

"Don't worry," she said. "You'll learn; so will Ziggy, won't you, Zig?" At the mention of her name, Ziggy jumped into Shelta's arms and purred like a kitten. My heart swelled as I looked at the two main loves of my life, and tears pricked my eyes as I cuddled them both. Ziggy licked both our faces in turn; she couldn't talk, but she could do the next best thing.

"My two angels," I said. "My hairy angel [I kissed Zig], and my golden angel." I kissed Shelta.

They both kissed me back, one on each cheek.

Shelta reached inside her jacket, pulled out a ring, and handed it to me. It was magnificent. It was a gold snake, coiled into a ring with blue stones inset as a pattern down its body and green eyes.

"It's called the Druid's Egg, and it's to bless our union. You gave me your egg and made our baby, so I give you mine."

At that moment in time, I loved her so much, it hurt. As we stood on the beach, the sun just started to rise, and we looked like we were standing on a distant planet, silhouetted against the sky.

“It’s fabulous,” I said as I put it on my ring finger. The eyes glowed blue and then back to green as it touched my skin, and a strange power flowed through me, a blue aura surrounding my frame.

“You are with the matrix now, De’Danann.” She bent down and kissed the ring on my finger. I felt like a god on Mount Olympus.

“Nice name,” I said. “Mr Taranis and Mrs Shelta-Thari De’Danann.” I took off my amulet and fastened the sheikh of Oman’s gold crest (the one Shelta wore as me) round her neck. “With this, I give you my heart, my life, my soul.”

Her eyes widened and glowed blue as tears trickled down her face, and her bottom lip trembled.

“Don’t cry baby, please,” I pleaded.

Poor little Ziggy jumped down from Shelta’s arms and did her “Please, please, please” trick as she looked back and forth at us.

“Taranis, we are blessed,” she said in a voice trembling with emotion.

“Please, Shelta, call me Kev till I get used to the other name.”

“Kev, oh Kev, we are blessed with the children of Ailill.”

“What’s that?” I asked, fear rigid in my throat.

“We don’t have a daughter, Kevin; we have twins: a girl and a boy.”

“Thank Taliesin we won’t have a hermaphrodite, then,” was the first thing that came to mind.

Ziggy jumped and barked as Shelta twirled round and round in ecstasy.

"This is the first time in three thousand years this has happened," she said, her face glowing with pride. "We are truly, truly blessed.

"Where did you get the amulet from?" she asked. "As soon as it touched me, the baby split to form two beings; it must be very powerful."

I explained how my mate George Hall did a special escort job for the sheikh and was given six amulets; he gave one to me as a token of friendship. I then had it blessed by my friend Peter Doyle's mother, who was of pure Romany blood.

"That's it," she cried happily. "Romany magic. Oh, Kevin, what a combination: the matrix, your powers, mine, the Romanies. It's a new beginning for a lot of people." She then frowned and added, "Apart from Toutaitis, or Zomolxis, as he is becoming. He will try to kill us and the children."

"Over my dead body," I shouted, grabbing my sword, unsheathing it with lightning speed, and going straight into the kill position.

I stood shaking with rage as Ziggy gave a low, deep growl as she stared out to sea. She had sensed something, and as I whirled round, ready to strike with Asmodeus, I saw a glint in the waves about eight hundred yards away. Shelta picked up Ziggy and cuddled her tight in her breasts to protect her, as we all noticed the rising sun bounce off an object in the water. The red and gold sky formed an eerie background as the sun rose. At first I thought it was a small submarine, but as my eyes focused, I saw the huge fin sticking up as it slowly cruised towards us.

I breathed in a huge sigh of relief and said, "It's only one of those basking sharks I told you about; they're harmless."

Ziggy's growl deepened as her hackles went up, and she bared her lethal fangs.

"Something's not right," Shelta said, and then a voice inside our heads boomed, *Beware the Ratapa and the Broichan sacrifice to Artemis.* Taliesin's voice was still echoing as we turned towards the sea.

What looked like a huge torpedo was racing towards us, and I got whacked as this huge mouth and gleaming red eyes appeared from beneath the waves. This was no basking shark but a great white, one of the most lethal killers in the world. Its eyes burned like two red suns, and its jaws widened into a huge black hole, exposing row upon row of razor-sharp teeth as it sped straight for us. Shelta was right: Toutaitis was exacting his revenge upon us.

"Go," I commanded. "You and Ziggy save yourselves; leave this motherfucking son of a Druid bitch to me." I stood watching this missile from hell come straight at us.

Shelta ran towards the cliffs, holding tightly onto Ziggy; she shouted back, "Have faith in the matrix, Taranis; have faith."

I'll never get used to that name, I thought as the shark got closer. I could almost smell its putrid breath. Its mouth was so big, it looked like it could swallow a car; I judged it to be about forty feet long as it sped towards me. Sand and sea spray burst up in the air as it hit the beach, sliding in towards me, mouth gaping. I flexed my leg muscles and bent down slightly as it snapped at me. I sprung up over its jaws and somersaulted onto the back of its head. I spread my legs and tensed them to get my balance and then shoved the blade into its neck, right up to the hilt, and pulled it straight back out, slicing down to one side as I did so.

The shark thrashed wildly, its huge tail going from side to side and forming a trench in the sand as the blade sliced into its gills. It wailed like a banshee as it gasped for breath, its whole body shaking as it went into its death throes. I was in a killing frenzy now, as the blood spurted out like red geysers. I went berserk with the blade; huge welts appeared on its body, exposing white tissue and bone as the blade slashed to and fro. The sand was awash with flesh, muscle, blood, and tissue as the beast screamed and screamed like a high-pitched siren echoing around the bay. My body was glowing with an electric blue light; it must have been an eerie sight to Shelta and Ziggy as they watched this carnival of horror.

I was in a complete trance, hypnotised into killing mode, but through the mists of my mind, I heard Ziggy barking and Shelta shouting, "Kev, Kev, its dead. It's dead; please stop."

As I stood there on top of the mountain of mutilated flesh, I awoke from my dreamlike state. I flew in the air like a gymnast, did a double somersault, and landed next to Shelta and Zig with the blade pointing away from them. The sun rose to its full extent on the horizon and shone on the dead carcass of the shark; steam rose as the day grew warmer. The stink was atrocious. The blue light dimmed as I returned back to my normal self, and I sat in the lotus position, sword across my legs.

Ziggy barked furiously at the shark's huge head as the red eyes dimmed. Its enormous jaw dropped shut, and the teeth clattered together; it was totally unexpected, and all three of us jumped with fright. I stared at the huge misshapen body; it seemed vaguely familiar. I couldn't see why it could be, so I shrugged the feeling off.

"By Taliesin, you were magnificent, Taranis." Shelta stopped and corrected herself: "Kevin, I mean."

"Why, thank you, ma'am," I replied in a Texan drawl, bowing to her.

Some sixth sense made me look up to the top of the cliff, and I saw a figure standing and pointing something at us. My sword and I were up in seconds, and I sprinted up the hill towards him. He dropped the item from his shoulder and waved, bemused. I stopped. He came walking towards me, and I noticed it wasn't a gun but a large zoom lens camera. I lowered my sword.

"Fabulous! Fabulous," he cried in an excited, Nancy boy voice. "Hi, my name's Ronnie. I work for the *Whitley Bay Guardian*. I came to take some shots of the lighthouse and St Mary's Island for a story we are doing when I saw that monster attack your party." He patted his camera. "Luckily I had this baby with me.

A thought crossed my mind, but Shelta answered me, *No, he won't have caught the blue light of the matrix on film. He will just think it's a trick of the light.*

Thank you, darling, I telepathised back. As I shook his hand, I said, "Hi, Ronnie; I'm Kev D'Arcy; this is Shelta-Thari De'Danann, and this is the one and only Ziggy."

He nodded back to all of us and said, "Pleased to meet you. This is the best scoop I've had in ages. I can't wait for the editor to see it. Kev, you're going to be a local celebrity. It's just like the film *Jaws,* and boy, did you carve that mother. Where did you learn all that?"

We went back down to the beach and sat on the blanket while I answered his questions.

Satisfied with all the answers, he said, "This is going to be the front-page story this Friday." His nose twitched with the putrid smell rising from the shark, now baking in the mid-morning sun. "Don't know what they're going to do with that," he added, pointing at the shark, "but the council should have some fun. Anyway, must get these developed. I'll meet you later; bye." He ran back up the hill.

“I need to get this blood and smell off me,” I said to Shelta as I handed her Asmodeus, jogged towards the water, and dived in.

Ziggy followed and splashed round beside me. We came back out of the sea; Ziggy shook herself dry, and Shelta handed me a towel. It felt good to get all the stinking stuff off as I rubbed myself vigorously with the towel. We sat quietly for a few moments as the sun shone and dried Ziggy and me off.

I turned to Shelta and said, “Toutaitis, I take it.”

“Well, yes, but not him personally. It’s the Broichan sacrifice to Artemis and one of the Rapata. The Broichan are Druid torturers who make sacrifices to nature, using Artemis as their evil god. He uses one of the Rapata as his everlasting minions to disfigure or kill you, using nature to do it.”

“I understand,” I said. “Is that what happened to Dorcas Tobias?”

“How did you know, Kev?” she asked.

“I don’t miss much, darlin’. I noticed the photograph of her, her husband, and her baby, and she was nothing like she is now, so I just put two and two together.”

“Toutaitis is getting even crueler as he transmogrifies into Zomolxis, and John Tobias is his right-hand man. Dorcas didn’t want to give up her baby, so when she passed the haunt, he returned to the human sphere and ensouled her unborn child. At the festival of the Samhain on the first of November, he gave her the wine of St Secaire’s mead, the Druids’ brew. Inside the goblet of the Dovaidona Magi Droata was a fly, and he was reborn from Dorcas’s womb. At the rebirth, he was a clone of himself. Sorry if this is all too complex.”

“No, I understand, but young John is a clone of his father, not Toutaitis.”

A bit puzzled, I shook my head.

She continued, “Toutaitis used Big John’s body for the clone to be bigger and more powerful in human shape; he used metempsychosis to get in the baby’s body to grow into Zomolxis; understand?”

“I do now. Those eyes on that baby were old and wise; they didn’t match the body, so he is the new Zomolxis, growing stronger each day.”

“Yes, yes, you’ve got it. You are obviously growing stronger too.” Ziggy yapped at Shelta’s heels. “Yes, you too, darling,” she said, patting her.

“I think I need a proper wash and shower after all this,” I said. “Let’s go.”

I gathered all the stuff and we headed up the cliff to the car. Even TBWSB looked as though she glowed with a blue light as I put the key in the lock. As I turned on the ignition, the dashboard lit up, and I switched on the rest of the machines, just in case there were any messages; there were. The clock on the dashboard said 7.03 and 26 seconds as I looked at the fax churning out a page.

“Dear Kev, please ring me,” it said, signed Graham Hood. “PS. It’s urgent.”

I dialled the number as Shelta looked on.

“Hi, Graham; it’s Kev. You all right? I see; okay, see you soon. Thanks for calling. I’ll ring you later. Bye.”

“Well, don’t keep us in suspense,” Shelta said. “What is it?”

“The hobbit; Graham said a motorist found him cut to bits; well, that’s what the authorities are saying, anyway.”

Stunned by what I had said, she replied, "So it was that horrible little gargoyle of a traffic warden? Well, he won't bother anyone any more, will he?"

"I knew I would see him again after that run-in at Graham's, but I didn't know he'd get so cut up about it," I quipped.

Wincing at the pun, she replied, "By Taliesin, Kev D'Arcy, you're a nutter. Doesn't anything ever bother you? You joke about everything, don't you?"

I smiled my wicked-little-boy smile at her and patted Zig on the head as I did so, but I was not smiling inside.

No, I don't joke about everything, I thought, *and I'm really scared. I don't want to lose you too.*

I looked towards Shelta, expecting a telepathised reply, but she just sat there, snuggling Ziggy as she looked out the window. I had just learned how to put my blocks against her, and this worried me.

Ziggy and Shelta dashed into the house, and I removed all the stuff from the boot and put it in the garage. After locking and alarming the car, I followed them. Shelta had lit the oven, and Ziggy was lapping up a bowl of milk as I entered the kitchen.

Ziggy turned her head and smiled at me, then went back to her milk, as Shelta, cracking eggs into a bowl, said, "Scrambled eggs on toast do you, while you go and shower?"

"You just read my mind," I said, laughing.

"I didn't before, though, do I?" I grimaced. "Don't worry," she said. "You are growing stronger, Kevin. A lot more than that will happen before this is finished. Just one thing, though: now that you can block your thoughts, please don't ever lie to me or deceive me. I couldn't stand that." A tear rolled down her cheek as she finished.

I brushed the tear away with my finger and kissed her forehead, wrapping my arms round her and cuddling her to my chest. I squeezed her tight, and lifted her head, and tilted it up to look at my eyes.

I gazed deeply into those pools of liquid green and said, "Let's have a party Friday night at the Lodge. I'll ask Gorgeous George if we can use the function room upstairs, if that's okay with you."

"What kind of party?"

"Well, first to celebrate our engagement [I twirled the ring she had given me]; secondly [I patted her stomach], to celebrate the birth of our children; and thirdly, to let you know I would never lie to you, Shelta-Thari De'Danann. I love you too much. I'm sorry about before, but I was really worried and scared. That's why the block must have come up."

Happy in that knowledge, she perked up and said, "Go get your shower, get dressed, and I'll have your breakfast ready when you come down."

"Okay," I said. "By the way, let's make it a vicars and tarts party; should be fun."

"Sounds interesting," she replied, "but let's do it the other way round. Girls do vicars and boys as tarts, to make it different."

As I ran up the stairs to the shower, I shouted back down to her, "I hope you're not thinking about mind mixing me into you again. I'll start thinking I'm turning into a girly."

As she stood at the oven, a strange lopsided grin appeared on her face.

Chapter 12

Welcome to the Pleasure Dome

After we ate, I said, "I must get on with some paperwork. Sending off proofs, checking contracts, and I have to bank the money I made."

"I'll take Ziggy for a walk and then tidy up the house," she said, looking round disapprovingly.

"Sorry, I don't spend much time here, but my mum comes in once a week to tidy up."

"No need to worry her. I'm going to be the new lady of the house now."

"Give me till about three o'clock, and then I'll take you down to see George and Brenda. I'll show you my dream."

"Your dream?" she asked.

As I pointed to my nose with my finger, I used her favourite trick and said, "You'll find out," and walked to my study.

Three o'clock on the dot, she was knocking on the door, and I could hear Ziggy scratching it at the same time.

"Afternoon, girls," I said as I opened the door. I picked up Ziggy and snuggled her in.

As the pup licked my face, Shelta said, "Me too," in a little girly voice. As I cuddled them both in, I felt like the happiest man on earth.

All of a sudden, my hi-fi switched itself on; strange, I hadn't set the timer. The light on the volume arced up to full power, and the spectrum analyser started flashing up and down as the karaoke system switched on. I watched the knob for the microphone go up to full, and a voice started booming out.

“Well, foolish ones, so you think you can beat me?”

Toutaitis, we both knew at once, and I could feel the pup shaking as she cowered.

“You destroy one Rapata minion, and you think you are gods. Well, you’re only babies, and talking of babies [A loud hissing sound came out of the speaker, and I watched Shelta double in pain], see how that feels, oh, mighty high priestess of Taliesin?”

My heart bled as I watched her writhe in agony.

“Hurt me instead of them, you piece of evil dog shit Druid,” I spat at the machine.

“Dog shit Druid? Well …”

The hissing started again; this time, Ziggy grimaced and jumped down. Her ears pricked up in fear, and her hackles rose. Her tail twitched, and she let go a loud fart and then sprayed diarrhoea all over the carpet.

“And what of you, Taranis? How about those amazing hands of yours?”

The hissing sounds came louder again.

My hands felt as though they were on fire, and something powerful grasped them.

“Welcome to the pleasure dome,” rasped out Toutaitis’s voice with a loud laugh. “Bet you’ve never heard Frankie Goes to Hollywood like this before." As the tape switched on, Frankie's version blasted out of the hi-fi, and all three of us writhed in agony.

Fucking great, I thought. *An evil bastard with an evil sense of humour.* I grimaced with pain and wondered how the hell I could stop him. It came to me like a dream: microphone 2 overrides microphone 1 and creates feedback. As the music continued, I made my way over to the hi-fi.

"No, no, I will not allow it," boomed out Toutaitis's voice.

"Eat my shit and die, dick head," I replied, turning up microphone 2, and a high-pitched hum like a scream emerged. The spectrum analyser reversed its display from down to up to down; the noise had overridden Toutatis, and the display was feeding back.

Just over the screeching sound, I heard him fading away as the voice was shouting, "No-o-o-o-o."

As it disappeared, so did our pain. The machine switched off, and we all gasped with the relief. Poor Ziggy looked at the mess she had made and whimpered. Shelta rubbed her stomach and back. My right hand looked as though it had been hit with a hammer. We composed ourselves, and Shelta took my damaged hands.

"It's okay," I said. "I have something for it." I showed her a special glove I had to help broken or arthritic bones and wrapped it round my hand.

"Amazing," she said. She tapped the glove; it echoed back. "What's that?"

"It has a metal strip in it for support, but it's also deadly if you hit someone with it."

"Jesus, it would break your face if it hit you."

"Exactly," I said.

"Well, since you're out of action, I'll tidy up the carpet," she said, looking at Zig's mess. "He's certainly trying every trick in the book to get us, isn't he?" she asked.

"Well, Toutatis, Zomolxis, or whatever you call yourself, I have a few tricks up my sleeve." I looked at the splint and tapped it.

"What are you going to do, Kev?"

"You'll see," I said, smiling, and she smiled back knowingly.

"No block that time. You're sly, Kev D'Arcy."

"I know, and that's what is going to beat that bastard," I replied, eyes twinkling as she went to tidy up the pup's mess while I made a phone call.

She came back just as I was saying, "Okay, Davy, that's great, and you'll tell Jack, the wagon driver? See you soon, mate. Bye."

"All done, then?" she asked, the pup sitting beside her.

I called Zig over and patted her rump: a sign that everything was all right, and she wasn't in the bad books.

"All done," I said. "Davy Bainbridge, electronics genius extraordinaire, and Jack Whitworth, the lorry driver, are going to help. Davy will supply all the electrical equipment, and Jack is borrowing a container and wagon. So Mr de la Wyle is in for a shock when the Geordie hit squad comes after him."

"Don't underestimate him, Kevin. He is very powerful and growing in strength daily."

"Don't underestimate the power of the Geordies," I replied, winking. I threw Shelta the keys to the car, looked at my damaged hands, and said, "You had better drive, under the circumstances."

"You're right," she said as we went to the car.

We drove along to Earsdon and turned right along to Holywell and went into Seaton Delaval. At Delaval, we turned right and headed down to Seaton Sluice, passing Delaval Hall on the way. As we approached, Seven Bellies rang me on the mobile.

"I need you back at Gretna Green, as there is a problem."

"Oh shit," I said. "That's an hour's drive to get back there." I told Shelta which way to go, and she changed directions and headed to my office.

She parked outside the office, and I went in to see Seven Bellies. When I got there, all it was, was the cheque from Fiona hadn't been signed.

"No problem," I said. "I can sort it out dead easy."

Shelta drove us back to Dornoch, where my eight-bedroom house is, and we ordered a slap-up Chinese meal from the Mystic Garden in Annan. I had my usual king prawn foo yung, fried rice, and chips, and Shelta had her favourite. What a feast. After eating, we went to our separate bedrooms for a good sleep, ready for another day.

Part 3

Chapter 13

I went back to Earsdon to pick up another cheque from Fiona, and she signed it.

Me, Shelta-Thari, and Ziggy headed up the A69 to Carlisle and then on to Dornoch. Three years ago, I won half a million pounds in the lottery and was able to buy an eight-bedroom Georgian mansion in Dornoch. It was run as a boutique hotel by my friends Gayle and Jason Taylor and their friend, Susan. Three of the bedrooms were for us; the other five were for guests. It was huge inside, very elegant, and business was very lucrative because of all the weddings held in the area.

Gayle managed the hotel, Jason was the chef, and Sue (known as Monkey) was the housekeeper. The large bedrooms had en-suites and walk-in wardrobes. My room was done up in a Chinese theme with black carpet and silver-white wallpaper that had black flowers on it. The room was filled with black and gold furniture and was very elegant.

Shelta and I dumped our things in the room, and Ziggy jumped on the king-sized bed. I turned the hi-fi on to listen to some music as we unpacked and then went to say hello to the staff and let them know what had happened. Jason made some sandwiches, and we sat and talked.

Shelta wasn't feeling well and asked me to go get some medication to help with the babies. Annan was only a few miles away, so I shot down to the local chemist's for some painkillers.

When I parked outside the chemist's, I noticed Toutaitis de la Wyle's big black Rolls-Royce across the road; the bastard must have followed us. Not good news. When I got back to the hotel and told Shelta, she was shocked. I needed to find out where he was and what he wanted.

Annan is a small town, and everyone knows about everything that goes on there. I found out he was staying in the big old mansion just outside of town and rang his mobile number to find out what he wanted.

"Hello, Kevin," he answered. "What can I do for you?"

"What do you want?" I asked.

"The babies," he said simply.

I was shocked and stunned.

"No way, you bastard," I replied.

"We'll see," he answered.

I didn't know how to tell Shelta, as I knew there was going to be big trouble.

She went berserk; I've never seen her so mad. Her eyes went black, and she began to shake, surrounded by a black aura. "I'll kill him," she said, over and over again.

I called Gayle; she was a fighter. Jason was a street fighter too, and Monkey was a little warrior. Gayle also had two pit bulls: Ellie, who was big and powerful, and Cookie, who was a cross-breed. I thought to myself, *I'm going to need all of them, because this is going to get nasty.*

We all went to be that night in a very subdued mood.

The next morning, when Shelta and I went downstairs for breakfast, there were four other couples in the dining room. Gayle brought us the breakfast Jason had cooked.

“Where’s Monkey?” I asked her.

“She went out early this morning with Ellie, because she was acting up again.”

We didn’t think any more of it. I needed to go see Seven Bellies in Gretna and was there all day.

When I got back around five o’clock, Gayle was crying.

“What’s wrong?” I asked.

“There’s still no sign of Monkey,” she replied, “so now I’m worried.”

We all went to bed about ten o’clock, and I was wakened at six the next morning by Gayle, screaming. I dashed downstairs, followed her voice into the back garden, and stopped in my tracks.

There in front of us were Monkey and Ellie, tied to a big oak tree; a cross had been placed inside of their bodies, growing through them, as though they’d been made into a tree. Their pain must have been unreal. Toutaitis de la Wyle had invoked a special Druid spell. This was a warning. We buried Monkey and Ellie, and then we all sat and cried.

He had invoked Derivest, the sacred race from the temple of Belenus. This meant we were going to have to face the Tetrachs, Druids, and priests (twelve bosses and three hundred minor village officials). This was monstrous; a total affront to my family and friends. The gloves were off now, and I had to go after Toutaitis.

Chapter 14

A New Beginning

There was another cry; this time, it was from Shelta-Thari, upstairs. I rushed, three stairs at a time, to our room. Her green eyes were bulging with pain. "The babies," she screamed. "The babies!"

Annan's ambulance station was only a few miles away, so I rang 9-9-9 and told them what was going on. They arrived in a few minutes. The paramedics came to the door, and I led them upstairs.

"She needs to go to hospital," I said. "The babies are coming early."

They took her downstairs, put her in the ambulance, and shot off to Dumfries Royal Infirmary. I followed behind in the TBWSB; thirty minutes later, we were there.

Shelta was rushed into maternity and was immediately admitted. Two hours later, the twins, a boy and a girl, arrived. We were ecstatic and called them Gabriella Shelta-Thari and Kevin Taranis De'Danann. We had kept Shelta's surname, since the babies were demigods. I thought they were going to be hermaphrodites.

I told Shelta "This is the first time in three thousand years this has happened, and these babies are going to be very powerful."

I was in awe of them; Gabriella was blonde with green eyes, and Kevin Jr was dark-haired with brown eyes. When I gazed at them, I thought, *You've been here before*, as they seemed to look straight into my soul.

Shelta was in hospital for three days and then came home to the hotel. I had purchased two beautiful cots and put them in our room;

perfect. Now the work would begin, as we had to protect the children at all costs.

I called my friend Anna Sorokin, the White Witch, to help. She came up from Cumbria to the hotel so we could tell here everything that was going on.

Chapter 15

And so, it began.

Anna assessed the situation and put a spell around the hotel and its grounds to protect us all. "If the spell is broken, I'll be here straight away to help," she said.

"We need to get them blessed as soon as possible," Shelta said.

"We can do it on June 22, the Druid summer solstice," I said. "It's only three weeks away. We can put up a big marquee in the back garden and invite all of our friends."

"Fabulous," said Shelta.

"Toutaitis must have learned about the babies by now," I said, as news travels fast around Annan, but nothing was happening. I asked Seven Bellies if I could take some time off to help with the babies, and he agreed. He wasn't all that bad, the fat twat.

The back garden was about an acre, so the marquee fit in no problem. Inside, we based everything on a Druid ceremony. We had a beautiful altar to bless the babies. There was seating for about a hundred people. The day came, and it was beautiful and sunny. Everyone came in wearing white robes. We stood at the altar, and I held Gabriella, while Shelta-Thari held Kevin, and they looked gorgeous, wide awake and alert in their little white robes. Anna Soronkin was reading the ceremony.

"*Ta mud anseo leis na deithe a adhradh*" ("We are here to honour the gods").

"Oh gods," she said, "whose power gives life to everything alive, be you here with us, rather than give us your presence."

I stood and faced everyone to say a prayer:

> I am bowing my head, in the eye of the Mother who gave me birth,
> in the eye of the Maiden who loves me,
> in the eye of the Crone who guides me in wisdom,
> in friendship and affection.
> Through the gift of nature, O Goddess,
> bestow upon us, fullness in our need.
> Love towards the Lady,
> The affection of the Lady,
> The laughter of the Lady,
> The passion of the Lady,
> And, the magic of the Lady,
> To do in the world Abred,
> As the ageless ones do in Gwnfyd;
> Each shade and light,
> Each day and night,
> Each moment in kindness,
> Grant us thy sight.

Everyone clapped, and the babies smiled at me and their mother.

We all started celebrating, and I passed the babies around, as it was their day. We were all laughing, joking, and carrying on, when in walked Toutaitis de la Wyle. Shock rang though the tent. He had six others with him.

Oh shit, I thought. *Trouble.*

The first thing I noticed was the huge figure next to Toutaitis; *John Tobias*, I thought. The rest were just gargoyles. Tobias changed into a Yeti-type creature; Toutaitis was half-wolf. He was what I saw on the road when I was attacked.

Iuatha, Shelta's mother, had come for the ceremony. I handed her the two babies to look after.

Anna Soronkin cast a spell over them to protect them. Gayle the Gladiator had her sword out, ready. Jason took up his boxing stance; Shelta had pulled her sword out as well.

I took out my sword, Asmodeus, ready to face the horde of demons. My friend Aizeen (the Huntress) had readied her bow to shoot. Shelta had told me that I had a dark angel that would protect me, Asera, so I called upon her. Shelta's dark angel was Taliesin, her real father; so she called upon him. When Toutaitis saw our numbers, he conjured up more demons.

All hell broke loose; people were screaming and body parts flying. Gayle went for Dorcas (John Tobias's wife) and sliced her into bits. Jason was punching the hell out of John Tobias. Aizeen was shooting arrow after arrow at the gargoyles, and they were dropping like flies; as I faced Toutaitis, I saw Gayle slashing away, killing everything in her path.

Both Taliesin and Asera appeared, killing everything they could lay they hands to. Carnage was everywhere. Toutaitis's eyes burned red when he saw me, and he ran towards the children.

Davy Bainbridge had installed generators and a huge Tesla coil on the grounds, for extra power. I told him to turn the coil on and lightning flashed all over as the power surged. I saw the fear in Toutaitis's eyes as the matrix began to appear. I lunged at this half-man, half-wolf figure and slashed at his right arm, cutting it off. His sword dropped. Screams and blood were all around, and the power began to surge through me and Shelta; we glowed an electric blue.

Toutaitis came at me like a whirlwind; his hand and arm had grown back.

"Oh, fuck," I exclaimed. Gayle and Shelta were slashing everything in sight; Aizeen was firing arrow after arrow at the gargoyles, and Jason had beaten John Tobias to a pulp.

Taliesin and Aresa stood next to Iuatha, Anna, and the babies, so that nothing could get at them.

The coil burned brighter and brighter and I felt my power increase. Our swords clashed heavy and hard as we battled. I had one more move I had learned in kendo and summoned all of my strength. The Tesla coil shot lightning bolts into me, and I glowed blue.

Toutaitis got a shock and stumbled back; I took my stance and slashed at him, cutting his right arm, then his left, and then his right and left legs. He stumbled as I slashed up between his legs, straight up, and then cut into his head as far as the sword would go. Green goo spurted from him everywhere, as he dropped to the floor.

"You're fucked now," I screamed.

A blue bolt shot over to him, and what was left of him disappeared in an explosion of light. All of his minions disappeared; it was all over. As I looked around, the carnage was unbelievable. Gayle, Jason, and Aizeen were all right; Anna and Iuatha were also okay. Taliesin and Aresa began to disappear. I saw Shelta running for the babies and followed her.

Chapter 16

2 October 1997

Today, I am forty-four years old; wow. Since the massacre, things had changed drastically.

News of the slaughter went nationwide, and the phone hadn't stopped ringing with folks wanting to book a room at the hotel. With Toutaitis gone, Shelta and Iuatha inherited his share of the George Hotel in Amesbury; they sold it for a million pounds and used the money to expand the hotel in Dornoch.

We built another fifteen double en-suite bedrooms, a bar, and a restaurant, as well as a conference centre. We made the back garden into a Japanese garden and erected a monument to Monkey and Ellie. We also put in an indoor pool, sauna, and gym. We left the Tesla coil as an ornament. Business was booming, and we'd booked up for a full year.

Shelta and I decided to live full-time in the hotel with the babies, so I sold my house in Whitley Bay and told Seven Bellies that I quit; he wasn't pleased. Shelta's cousin, Justine, got the priory and sold it, moving up here to start a high-end antique business. She'd wanted to specialise in Chinese and Japanese furniture, the things I loved. She was having a huge showroom built right next door to the hotel, so we could all be together. Life was good.

I decided to propose to Shelta at my birthday party. Asera, my dark angel, had sent me a vision of Stonehenge; on the altar stone was a pregnant sixteen-year-old, who was about to be sacrificed. As they were about to strike with the knife, she sat up and began to turn electric blue; lightning bolts shot from her fingers, destroying the priests. Then it hit me; that girl was me, three thousand years ago.

This is why I was so close to the Druids. I told Shelta about this, and she told me she already knew. This was the reason we'd bonded straight away.

Anna Sorokin had made a unit for herself at the hotel called the Secret Tarot Garden, where she read tarot cards and practiced her magical arts. Aizeen took the place of Monkey, so things were going well for all of us.

I decided to go and get ready for my birthday party but went to see the babies first. They lay smiling away at me, and then the strangest thing happened: They were surrounded by an electric blue light, and then, right before my eyes, Gabriella transmogrified into Kevin, and he did likewise, into Gabriella.

"Oh, my God," I shouted at Shelta.

"And so it begins," she responded. But that's another story.

The End

(or is it a new beginning?)

www.ingramcontent.com/pod-product-compliance
Lightning Source LLC
Chambersburg PA
CBHW030413310726
48979CB00002B/394
* 9 7 8 1 9 5 3 3 9 7 2 4 9 *